DETROIT PUBLIC LIBRARY
W9-ADQ-575
3 5674 ... 5

1/03

PA

A Circle of Time

A Circle of Time

MARISA MONTES

Parkman Branch Library
1766 Oakman Blvd.
Detroit, Mich. 48238

A TIME TRAVEL MYSTERY

HARCOURT, INC.
San Diego New York London

Copyright © 2002 by Marisa Montes

All rights reserved. No part of this publication may be reproduced or transmitted in any form or by any means, electronic or mechanical, including photocopy, recording, or any information storage and retrieval system, without permission in writing from the publisher.

Requests for permission to make copies of any part of the work should be mailed to the following address: Permissions Department, Harcourt, Inc., 6277 Sea Harbor Drive, Orlando, Florida 32887-6777.

www.HarcourtBooks.com

Library of Congress Cataloging-in-Publication Data
Montes, Marisa.
A circle of time/Marisa Montes.
p. cm.
Summary: In 1996, a fourteen-year-old girl in a coma is forced back in time by a girl who died in 1906, and who needs help in righting a series of terrible wrongs.
[1. Time travel—Fiction. 2. Will—Fiction. 3. Family problems—Fiction. 4. Spanish Americans—Fiction. 5. Coma—Fiction. 6. California—History—1850–1950—Fiction.] I. Title.
PZ7.M76365Ci 2002
[Fic]—dc21 2001002614
ISBN 0-15-202626-6

Text set in Sabon
Display set in Goudy Catalogue
Designed by Cathy Riggs

First edition
A C E G H F D B

Printed in the United States of America

To my soul mate and husband,
David Plotkin:
I've known you before,
and I know we'll meet again,
in our own circle of time

SPECIAL THANKS to my aunt, Dr. Carmín Montes Cumming, for being my Spanish-language consultant and for always encouraging me to write, and to my brother-in-law, Dr. Fred Plotkin, Board Certified in both Emergency Medicine and Preventive Medicine, for lending me his medical expertise and for making sure my medical scenarios were as realistic as possible.

Thanks also to my critique-group members, Corinne Hawkins and Debbie Novak, for their suggestions and encouragement; to my mentor Barbara A. Steiner, for being my eager audience during each partial installment of the rough draft of this novel; and especially to my editor, Karen Grove, for showing me how to add another dimension to my story.

IN THE MISTS OF TIME

by Marisa Montes

Like ghosts, true love is talked about;
but only few have little doubt
that either one on Earth exists.
So I am blessed: For in the mists
of time, I have found you.

Mere words cannot express the joy
that even time cannot destroy:
the depth, the passion that I feel.
Yet earthly death has dared to steal
your body from my soul.

I cannot rest; life's lost its thrill.
I need you back—I'll fight, I'll kill!
I'll battle death; I'll travel time,
for mere existence is a crime.
Dear God, please, take me, too!

The past dissolves into the now.
I take a chance. Will fate allow
the two of us to meet again?
But oh, if so—no matter when—
your love, I shall extol!

Past life and death, I shall transcend
to search for you till heaven's end:
At first, he's someone I don't know—
Until, within his eyes . . . that glow . . .
I recognize—*He's you!*

PROLOGUE

Devil's Drop

April 18, 1996

LIGHTNING SLASHES THE BLACK SILK NIGHT. RAIN pelts the winding mountain road. Gusts of wind slap a tiny Honda back and forth across the slippery road the way a cat teases a small rodent before devouring it.

In the middle of the road, a teenage girl in an old-fashioned calico dress watches the approaching car. She waits, sensing the movements of the woman inside the Honda.

The woman squints against the glare of the headlights shimmering on the pavement. Weak windshield wipers flop from side to side, useless against the pounding rain. She grips the steering wheel, tensing her muscles as she concentrates on the wall of water.

Approaching a sharp curve, she taps the brakes. The road is getting steeper, and she's nearing Devil's Drop. Despite the cold night, perspiration begins to form on her neck and forehead. Her hands, still glued to the steering wheel, become slippery with sweat.

As she makes the sharp V turn of Devil's Drop, the Honda skids and begins to fishtail. A bolt of lightning reveals a figure standing frozen in the road. The woman's heart smacks her rib cage. She steps on the brakes, skidding to a stop only inches from the girl, so close she can see the girl's odd eyes, pale and luminous as moons.

The girl's blond braids drip with rain. Her calico dress is plastered to her slim body. The headlights give the girl an eerie glow. She raises an arm and points toward the rocky shoulder of the road. Another flash of lightning reveals a bicycle crumpled against the dented metal barrier.

"What the—" The woman flings herself out the door and is shoved against the car by a giant gust of wind. Icy knives of rain slash her face. When the woman regains her balance, the girl in the calico dress is gone.

The woman staggers to the metal barrier, fighting spiraling currents of wind and rain. Another bolt of lightning flashes. She sees the girl kneeling beside the twisted body of another girl midway down the ravine, on a narrow ledge.

"Oh, my god!" she cries. "Don't move! I'll get help." The woman returns to her car and calls for an ambulance. "Highway One, Devil's Drop. One girl injured...maybe two...Please, hurry!"

The girl in the calico dress caresses the forehead of the still form, gently pushing aside clumps of rain-soaked hair. An ugly gash, still oozing blood, is visible at the hairline. Her face is bruised, badly scraped, and streaked with blood, dirt, and rain.

"Don't worry," the girl whispers. "I'll take care of you...and you'll take care of me."

The girl begins to glow, softly at first, like the delicate light of a birthday candle, then with more intensity. She envelops the unconscious girl's body with her light, becoming one with her. Then, as though extinguished by a puff of wind, the glowing light vanishes.

PART ONE

The Coma

Like ghosts, true love is talked about;
but only few have little doubt
that either one on Earth exists.
I am blessed: For in the mists
of time, I have found you.

CHAPTER I

I'm wrapped in darkness, and a warm tingling travels through my body. I feel so light, so light, as if I'm floating. Something behind me goes *swish-swush, swish-swush,* and to my right, there's a faint *beep, beep, beep*...

Is someone there? I can barely make out soft, muffled voices. I try to turn my head to see who it is, but my head won't move, and my eyes won't open.

The voices come closer. *Mom? Mommy!* I cry out.

What's happening? Something's wrong. My lips seem glued together...they won't—can't?—move!

What is that? I hold my breath, trying to sift out the tiniest sound. Someone is sobbing, and a voice says something that sounds like "coma." Now the voices move farther away. I'm floating again—this time up, up, high above a tiny room.

I can see them now. It's Mom, bent over, shoulders shaking, hands covering her eyes. A woman in a white lab coat places an arm over Mom's shoulders. They're watching a girl who's lying pale and still on a small bed.

Tubes run in and out of the girl's body and are

connected to machines behind her and at her side. Bandages cover her skull, and her left arm and leg are encased in plaster. I glance quickly around the room. It's cold and barren except for the bed, a curtain hanging from a track on the ceiling, a tray table near the girl's feet, and a straight-backed chair tucked in a corner. The curtain is drawn shut and flutters in the breeze from the heater vent located beneath the window.

I look back at the pale girl in the bed below. Why is Mom staring at her like that? What is she to her? And why does she look so familiar? Her face is so scratched and bruised and swollen, but there's something familiar… something…

Oh, my god! Oh, my god—Mommy! It's me! The girl on the bed—it's me!

Lightning flashes. Thunder. A force I can't fight yanks me up, pulling me through the ceiling. Another flash of light, and the room and my mother vanish—

Mo-o-ooom!

But the scream is ripped from my throat as I'm sucked through darkness down a tunnel of wind toward a bright, rosy light. Before I can struggle against the strong tug, I drift down into a sunlit meadow filled with golden California poppies.

The air smelled of freshly moistened earth and grass. Cool raindrops dripped from the tall weeds onto her bare legs and feet and wet the hem of her dress as she walked. Despite the clear sky and bright sun, the air felt chilly, like in the early days of April when spring is still trying to convince winter that it has arrived.

Allison Blair reached up to pull her sweater around her chest, when she realized she was wearing only a thin calico dress that she didn't remember owning. It couldn't be hers—the dress fit awkwardly across the waist and shoulders, and it was a dumpy, old-fashioned style. What was she doing wearing this thing? Where were the comfortable blue jeans and T-shirt she was wearing when she left home this morning? Come to think of it, where was she?

Allison scanned the thick row of pine trees that encircled the meadow. Directly in front of her, and where her feet seemed to be heading, sat a rough log cabin tucked under tall pines.

Somewhere behind her, a voice called, "Becky! Becky, wait up!"

Allison turned. A tall boy emerged from the pines. He ran toward her, jumping over fallen trees and branches, his curly, sun-bleached brown hair flopping up and down as he ran. He wore baggy, ragged pants, a faded plaid flannel shirt, and he, too, was barefooted.

"Becky, you're late," he said. His gray eyes danced with mischief.

Allison backed away from the boy. "I'm not—"

"Stop playing, Becky." The boy gave her an impish grin. He tugged one of her braids, drawing her toward him. "Come on back before your mama sees."

Allison lifted her hand to touch the thick, honey-blond braids that hadn't been there this morning, but the boy grabbed her arm and pulled her toward the thicket of pines. Allison was too stunned to resist. Besides, despite his shabby clothes, he had to be the cutest boy she'd ever seen.

She let the boy lead her into the pines. As they entered

the thicket, a woman's shrill voice shattered the peaceful silence. "Rebecca Lee! Come on home, now. Rebecca!"

"Oh, Becky—I told you we wouldn't have time." The boy hung his head. Allison noticed that he didn't look as old as she'd first thought. He was so tall that she'd thought he was about sixteen or seventeen. But he didn't seem mature enough. He was probably fifteen or fourteen, like Allison.

The boy turned her toward the cabin. "You'd better git, or she'll find out about us."

Allison didn't want to go. "But I'm not—"

"Don't argue, Becky. Remember what happened last time?"

"Rebecca!" The woman was getting closer.

"I'd better scat, Becky." The boy turned and ran into the woods. "Same time, same place, next week—this time don't be late!"

Before Allison could reply, he disappeared behind a clump of trees. She stared, wondering whether she'd imagined his playful smile, when a hand hit her shoulder and flung her around.

"Rebecca Lee Thompson! Here you are again, daydreaming. You haven't been wasting time thinking about that no-good Joshua Winthrop, have you?" The woman grabbed Allison's arm and pulled her toward the house. "Don't you care that we have to be at the estate early tomorrow, and you still haven't finished sewing Miz Teresa's dress?"

Allison jerked back, forcing the woman to face her. "Look, I'm not—"

A powerful hand slapped Allison across the face, drawing blood. "Don't you ever take that tone with me, you hear? Now, move!"

Too terrified to resist further, Allison let the woman drag her across the meadow. As they were nearing the cabin, Allison became aware of a faint voice, as soft as a whisper in the wind, traveling over the meadow and through the pines: "Allison? Allison, please wake up, sweetheart."

"Mom!" Allison tried to wrench her arm free. "Mommy, help me!"

"I'll help you all right," said the woman beside her, refusing to loosen her grip. Instead, the woman used her free hand to give one of Allison's braids a sharp tug, sending waves of needle-sharp pain throughout her scalp. Allison stopped struggling and let herself be dragged toward the cabin.

"Allison," the voice called again.

Drawing strength from the voice, Allison yanked her arm free from the woman's grasp. She bolted. Tall weeds ripped and scratched her legs as she tore across the meadow, crying, "Mommy, help me!"

"Allison, wake up," the voice pleaded.

As Allison ran, she could feel herself lifting from Becky Thompson's body and floating into the air. In the meadow below, she could see a girl in a calico dress running, tripping, and falling, while a large, heavyset woman caught up with her and struck her again and again about the head. Then, the girl and woman were gone, and Allison was in the wind tunnel, speeding toward a white light.

I'm a feather, floating down to earth, alighting on a bed.

Mom's beside me, holding my hand. I feel warm and relaxed. I sigh. It was only a dream, a nasty nightmare.

Then I hear what she's saying; I focus on Mom's voice. She's pleading with me, begging me to open my eyes.

My heart flutters. I try to do what she asks. *I'm trying, Mom. I'm trying!* my mind screams. But as much as I try, my head won't turn, and my eyes refuse to open.

Mom, help me! Please, help! I can't move!

Then a thought consumes me—a thought too horrible to bear: Somehow, someway, my body has become a coffin, lid shut tight, trapping me inside.

I'm buried alive in my own body!

CHAPTER 2

Outside, the storm rages. Thunder rumbles through my bones. The curtains must be open because I can sense lightning rip the air just outside the window. My mind starts at the sound—I want to scream and cover my face—I've always been terrified of lightning.

I try to pull the sheets over my head. But my arm lies limp at my side, as if the signal my brain is sending—telling my arm to move—is dissolving, evaporating, leaving my body before it ever reaches my arm.

My heart gives a sharp kick. *Am I paralyzed?*

Maybe it's just my arm. I try my hand, then a finger. Now I try my other arm, now a leg, a toe. I concentrate on trying to sit up, and I realize my eyes are still closed. I try to move my eyes, to open my eyelids. But each part of my body refuses to obey my commands.

The word *coma* fills my mind. Someone, earlier . . . today? . . . yesterday? . . . said "coma." Referring to me?

Bits and pieces of memory return. Images bombard my brain: a woman in a white lab coat, hugging Mom; Mom calling my name, holding my hand. A floating sensation.

A meadow. A boy. Machines *swish-swushing* and *beep-beep-beeping.* Getting ready for school Thursday morning...

I chose my favorite blue jeans with the rip above the right knee and my faded SAVE THE RAINFORESTS T-shirt. When I had finished throwing on my clothes, I shoved my books into my backpack and headed for the kitchen.

"Mom," I said, giving her a quick peck on the cheek, "I'm late. Could you pour some granola in a Baggie? I'll munch on it when I get to school."

"Dry?" Mom made a face.

I gave her one of my "Mother, puh-leeze" looks.

"I like it that way," I told her, raising an eyebrow, suggesting that I was in no mood for an argument. Then I took a sip of orange juice, and when Mom handed me the Baggie of granola I slipped it into my backpack and started for the door.

"Can't you at least finish your juice?"

"Mom, I'm late. And I'll be late tonight. It's April eighteenth, remember?"

Mom gave me a blank stare.

"My interview at the rangers' station."

"Oh," Mom said, "be care—"

I didn't wait to hear the rest. I ducked into the garage and rolled my bike to the driveway. As I was about to climb on the bike, Mom darted out the front door.

"Allison, your helmet."

"Oh, Mom..."

"It only takes a second to put it on, sweetheart. There. Now be careful on that mountain road—"

"Gotta go, Mom—I'm late!" I swung my leg over the bike and rolled into the street.

"Late, late, late," I muttered, checking my watch.

"Late, late, late," says the White Rabbit as he checks his pocket watch. He slips into the rabbit hole and begins to fall down, down, down a dark tunnel. "I'm laaaaate..."

Now *I'm* falling down the tunnel. Floating, falling, floating...allowing myself to be propelled along. I land in a meadow. The smell of fresh, rain-soaked earth invades my senses; the crisp spring day caresses my skin.

Images form again, flashing in my brain like the flickering scenes of a silent movie: I see a cabin; a boy running; tall pine trees, towering; a woman pulling me...her?... pulling who? I'm running. I'm floating. I'm lying limp in a strange bed.

What's happening to me? my mind screams. *Somebody, please help me!*

"Shh-hh...," a voice whispers. "I'll help you. Don't you fret none. I'll help you, and you'll help me."

Who's there? Who said that? Can you hear me?

"I can hear you. Don't you fret." The voice is fading.

Can you help me?

"I can help you." The voice is barely audible. "And you can help me."

Lightning flashes, electrifies the air. I feel myself rising from the bed and floating above it. I remember, now—I remember the last time this happened!

No! I don't want to go! Please, don't—

A sudden wind lifts me up, envelops me, and whirls me through a long tunnel toward a rosy light.

Noo-ooo!

She was consumed with terror. A desperate need to run, to escape imminent danger, kept her legs pumping, running blindly.

Branches reached out and ripped her face as she tore through the forest. Her heart, throbbing, throbbing, felt as though it would explode. Her lungs burned, her legs ached. But she knew she could not stop running. Whatever was chasing her grew closer.

She could hear its chest heaving, rasping, struggling to suck in more air, and branches slapping and breaking as they hit the approaching force. Or was it *her* breath she heard, *her* body against which branches slapped and broke? She couldn't stop to find out.

She crashed through a final crowd of branches and stopped at the edge of a clearing. Her throat was dry. Her limbs trembled from overexertion. She bent forward to ease the painful stitch in her side. A thin stream of moonlight illuminated the calico dress.

It was smeared with dark stains. She held up her hands. They felt gooey, sticky. She sniffed. Her stomach lurched as her brain recognized the smell.

Blood.

She was covered in blood!

"Allison, sweetheart, I'm here. Allison..."

Mom's voice draws me back through the wind tunnel. I see the tiny room below me, and I feel the pressure of the bed as I sink into my body.

The warmth of Mom's hand feels good, safe. I will my fingers to curl around Mom's, but they refuse to obey.

Mom strokes my cheek. "I tried to get back as soon as

I could. I know how you hate to be alone during thunderstorms. But I closed the curtains—to keep out the lightning. Can you tell?"

Warm, moist lips touch my forehead. I breathe in the faint scent of Mom's tea-rose perfume mingled with French-roast coffee. My mind relaxes, lets go, releases the fear and dread of whatever is happening to me. For the first time since this nightmare began, I feel safe.

Don't move, Mommy. Stay close. Hold me.

As if she can hear my thoughts, Mom says, "You know I'd stay here twenty-four hours a day if I could, sweetie. My heart breaks each time I leave this room with you lying here"—her voice catches—"like this..."

Mom rests her head against my side and holds me. She begins to sob.

Even as the strong tug rips me from my body, my mind yells, *Don't cry, Mom. I'm trying to come back. I'm trying!*

CHAPTER 3

Something hard and cold pressed against Allison's forehead. Her back ached. Slowly, she opened her eyes and lifted her head. In front of her stood an old-fashioned sewing machine, its metal body crouched before her on its wooden stand like a giant black cricket. Allison's head had been resting on its cold metal back. She rubbed the painful dent the metal had left on her forehead. Still dazed, Allison glanced around.

The room was silent. A musty odor mingled with the thick, greasy smell of cooked lamb hung heavily in the air. Her eyes took in the rough wooden table and four chairs pushed under a tiny window framed with ragged curtains. A black cast-iron stove squatted next to a wooden counter that supported an iron water pump. To Allison's left, a curtain had been pushed back, exposing a bed covered with a faded quilt. Above it, a crude ladder led up to a shadowy loft.

Her heart began to pound. Where was she? She spun around to look behind her. A stone fireplace covered most of the back wall. In front of it, an old wooden rocker sat between a woodpile heaped on the hearth and a basket brimming with coarse yarn. The only source of light was the single window in the kitchen.

Allison felt as if she were a wax figure in the museum display of a log cabin she'd seen last year when her eighth-grade history class had taken a field trip to Sacramento. Was this another of those bizarre dreams she'd been having? One minute she'd find herself in a hospital bed unable to move, her mother sobbing at her side, and the next minute she'd be in another time and place—a time and place totally alien to her—and in another girl's body. Nightmares from which there was no escape.

Allison looked down. She groaned. She was wearing Becky Thompson's faded calico dress. She looked at her feet: They were bare and propped on the wide wrought-iron pedal of the sewing machine. She lifted a trembling hand to her hair—it was braided—two long, blond braids. Allison was a brunette with chin-length hair, and she didn't own a calico dress.

Then it hit her—this must be the rough cabin in the woods she saw the first time she was in Becky's body. And if it was, Becky's horrible mother would be back any minute.

Allison jumped from the chair and bolted for the door. The latch was awkward, stiff. She fiddled with it. Her heart pounded fiercely. Her whole body shook. Finally, the latch let go. Allison threw open the door and froze.

She was staring into the angry eyes of Becky Thompson's mother.

"And just where do you think you're going?" The heavyset woman shoved Allison back into the room and placed a basketful of eggs on the table. She turned to the sewing machine. "You ain't going anywhere till you finish that dress we promised Miz Teresa for next week. How far have you gotten?"

The woman lumbered to the sewing machine, boots hitting *clomp! clomp! clomp!* beneath her long cotton skirt. She picked up the piece of rose chiffon that was still attached to the needle, eyed it with displeasure, and let it drop. Then she sorted through other pieces of the same fine fabric folded in a large straw basket next to the sewing machine.

"That's it?" Mrs. Thompson turned, her face contorted with rage. "One sleeve—that's all you've done this morning?"

Allison stared at the woman in confusion, her eyes wide with terror. In one mighty leap, the woman was towering over her. Drawing back her arm, she struck Allison across the face with the back of her hand, propelling her against the wall. Pain shot through her entire body; her mind was a blur. Allison could taste blood. Her knees quivered.

"You stupid, lazy girl! I'll teach you to daydream when you should be working!"

Mrs. Thompson pulled back a closed fist, aimed directly at Allison's face, and let go. An explosion of pain and colors and flames burst inside Allison's head. Then the burning pain and brilliant colors faded to black, and Allison was back in the wind tunnel, whirling toward a voice.

At first, the voice seems muffled and far away, as if it's in another room and I'm listening through the wall. Slowly, the voice clears, and I can make out the words.

". . . The nurse brought me a cot so I can stay with you at night. And I brought your boom box so the nurses can play your favorite music for you when I'm at work."

Mom! Oh, Mom, help me out of this nightmare! I've got to get out of here.

I can hear Mom moving around the room as she talks. Paper crackles. Now she's next to my bed. "And look what else I brought. Feel."

Mom places something soft and light on my arm, resting it against my shoulder. "Recognize it? It's PoPo, your old teddy bear. I found him in the back of your closet. Remember how you always made me drag him out when you were sick?"

Thunder crashes outside the window.

PoPo? Good old PoPo... Can you keep me safe?

CHAPTER 4

Outside, the storm continues to roar.

Inside, my mind struggles to think, to remember what it was that put me in this bed, in this state of half life. Maybe, if I could only remember, maybe the knowledge could give me a clue to unlock the door that keeps my mind and body apart. Even a tiny clue. I just need *something* to give me hope that this nightmare can end.

But more and more, I seem to be drifting between light and dark, active thoughts and silence, clear images and nothingness. It seems harder to keep my mind awake, harder to hear Mom speak. The music from the boom box fades in and out. My hold on life seems to be slipping. *I've got to hold on! I've got to—*

"Allison, can you hear me? Allison? The lady who found you at Devil's Drop just called to find out how you're doing. Isn't that nice, darling? She's called every day since the accident. Such a nice lady..."

Mom sighs. "So unlike the monster who did this to you. The police haven't found him yet..."

My legs ached from pumping uphill against the wind. The higher I rode up Mountain Road, the stronger and faster the wind blew, fighting me every inch of the way. It whipped my hair about my face and made my eyes tear.

Gray-black clouds, angry and menacing, covered the sun, stealing the precious afternoon light. I muttered to myself as I struggled to pump harder, faster, to make up lost time. I squinted and blinked against the wind and the bits of dust it carried.

My arms trembled with the strain of trying to keep the bike from weaving on the bumpy pavement and the front wheel from skidding onto the soft, gravel shoulder. Maybe this was a mistake. The mountain was windy under normal conditions. I usually enjoyed it, but this was too much. What was going on? A storm brewing?

Should I turn around and go home?

But I've worked so hard to get this interview! If I make the cut, I can do a summer internship with the forest rangers. I'd kill for the chance! No, *I have to keep going. What kind of forest ranger would wimp out at the first sign of a little wind? That would make a great impression.*

As I approached the sharp V of Devil's Drop, I heard the screeching of tires. The moment I started to pull over, to let the car pass, a bright red sports car careened around the bend, aimed directly at me.

In that split second, time seemed to stand still. My brain registered the fact that the car was my favorite make—an older model Mercedes-Benz 450 SL. The top of the convertible was down, and the look on the young man's face mirrored my horror. Memories flew at me: I'd been too preoccupied that morning to hug Mom good-bye. As I rode away from school that afternoon, my friend Jenny warned me not to ride up Mountain Road because a storm was brewing. And when the car hit my bike, crashing it into the metal barrier, and as I flew over the cliff to the ledge below, I remembered I wasn't wearing my helmet.

My helmet! I hit my head on a rock. That's why I'm here. I really am *in a coma. I've kept thinking this is a nightmare, and I just have to wait till morning.*

But now I know what I have to do to wake up. I have to fight. I can't just lie here and wait. I have to fight!

I struggle to stay alert, to hear Mom's words, to hear the music from the boom box, but my mind feels heavy, sluggish. I'm sinking down, down into a dark hole. The image of the White Rabbit falling down the rabbit hole returns.

No! I have to wake up! Mom, help me. Talk to me. Bring me back!

"Sorry, Allison, but it's time."

Time for what? Who is that?

"Time for you to help me, Allison. I helped you. I made sure you was brought here. Now you can get help from them docs and your mama. I helped you, now you help me."

You helped me? Can you help me now?

"Later, Allison. I'll help you again, later. But first, it's my turn. First, you got to help me."

Please, help me wake up. Then I'll do whatever you ask.

"Can't do that. Only way's you can help me is if you

go where I send you now. That means you can't wake up yet."

No, I don't want to go anywhere. I—

"Don't worry, Allison. I'll stay here and keep your ticker tickin'. I'll help you, and you'll help me."

In my mind's eye, I see the dingy log cabin and Becky's horrid mother. *Please, I don't want to go back there. I'll do anything else . . .*

But my voice is swept away by the strong winds that carry me down the long tunnel and toward the rosy light.

PART TWO

The Other

Mere words cannot express the joy
that even time cannot destroy:
the depth, the passion that I feel.
Yet earthly death has dared to steal
your body from my soul.

CHAPTER 5

"Becky Lee? Bequita, are you all right?"

Allison awoke to the fragrance of roses. "Mom?" It was the first word that entered her head, and without thinking, she spoke it out loud.

Laughter that sounded like wind chimes tinkling in a passing breeze filled her ears. The sound made Allison suddenly aware that she was in a room, kneeling on cold ceramic tile. Tucked beneath her knees was the hem of Becky Lee Thompson's calico dress.

"Where is your mind, *niña*?" The laughing voice came from somewhere behind her. Allison turned. She was met with a brilliant smile and sparkling blue eyes. The young woman laughed again. "You have been daydreaming all afternoon. Your *mamá* left half an hour ago."

My mama? She must mean Becky's horrible mother. Just as well she's gone.

Allison nodded. "Yes, yes, of course. I was just—"

"No need to explain." The young woman tilted back her head, swishing long chestnut curls behind her. "If a boy looked at me the way Joshua Winthrop looks at you,

I would confuse old Paco, there, with my *papá.* After all, they both have the same head of bushy white hair, so who could blame me?"

Allison glanced where the woman had pointed with her chin. In the corner of the large room, an ancient sheepdog lifted his head, sniffed the air blindly, and lay its massive head back on his paws.

"*Qué bello,* Bequita. You've done a marvelous job on this dress." The young woman spun before a full-length mirror, causing the skirt of the long chiffon dress to spread open like a parasol. "And the dusty rose brings out the pink in my cheeks and sets off my eyes, no?"

"Umm, yes." Allison couldn't help wondering who this lovely young woman was. She was probably in her early twenties. And rich. *Very, very rich,* Allison thought, as her eyes scanned the huge bedroom suite.

Early Spanish design and decor, she guessed. Terracotta tiles around the fireplace, expensive woven area rugs on the slick tile floor, carved four-poster bed with matching nightstands and wardrobe, a sitting area furnished with heavy mahogany furniture. Religious items softened the heaviness of the dark furniture: A jewel-studded gold cross hung above the bed, surrounded by golden icons of Madonna and child, while statuettes of the Virgin Mary and various saints populated the nightstands. Vases of roses were scattered everywhere—on the low coffee table, on the mahogany mantel, on the nightstands, on the windowsills, even on the steps leading up to the French doors.

The woman stopped spinning and turned. "Here, Bequita, let me help you up so you can admire your handiwork."

Allison was still kneeling on the floor, next to a sewing kit. The woman took Allison's right hand and pulled. The motion sent searing waves of pain up Allison's arm. She jerked back and cried out.

"Becky, what happened? Did I pull too hard?"

"No, I—I don't know...You didn't pull that hard..." Allison stood, still cradling her right arm.

"Here, let me." The young woman held Allison's arm. Gently, she pushed up the long calico sleeve.

"*¡Dios mío!* Becky, this is horrible."

Allison gasped at what she saw. Ugly purplish bruises formed the clear prints of a large hand on Becky's—now Allison's—forearm. Reddish-brown scrapes indicated skin burns from the twisting of flesh in opposite directions. Gingerly, Allison felt her upper arm. She winced.

"It hurts there, too?"

Allison nodded. Her eyes blurred with tears, and a lump formed in her throat at the sound of the woman's caring voice. In a strange time and place, far, far from home, she felt so vulnerable that any bit of kindness was touching. The pain Becky's body felt was nothing compared to what Allison's spirit was feeling. She didn't trust herself to speak, for fear she'd break down blubbering.

"I do not have to ask who did this to you." The woman's voice had become hard and indignant. "That woman should be horsewhipped. If I could, I would—"

"No, please." Allison slipped her sleeve back over her arm, covering the evidence of violence. "I appreciate your kindness. But I don't know what else she might do."

"*Sí, sí.* Of course, you are right. But if you ever need

anything. Remember, you can trust me. Teresa Cardona Pomales is nothing if not trustworthy." Teresa tilted her chin upward in a gesture that conveyed both haughtiness and quiet dignity.

From the few moments she'd spent in the woman's presence, Allison believed her. She felt secure that this woman, whoever she was, was someone to be trusted. But could she be trusted with Allison's secret? What would Teresa Cardona Pomales think if Allison confessed that she wasn't really Becky but a girl from the future imprisoned in Becky Lee Thompson's body?

Her thoughts were interrupted by the loud *bang* of the heavy double door bursting open. Through the door strode a tall man with a wild mop of white hair. "Tere, where have you been?"

The man spoke Spanish, but Allison had studied the language in school, and as long as the person spoke clearly and deliberately, she could make out what was said. And this man spoke *very* deliberately.

"Don Gutiérrez and I have been waiting at least half an hour—finally he had to go. He brought the young mare and"—the man lowered his voice—"he was anxious to meet you."

The man's hair reminded Allison of a picture she'd seen of Albert Einstein—pure white and flying straight out on the sides. Despite the white hair, the man had the rugged features and physique of a younger man. His presence dominated the large room, seeming to shrink it to half its size.

Teresa did not appear impressed. She shook her long curls and gave an annoyed sigh. "Papá," she replied in

Spanish, "I have no interest in Don Gutiérrez or any of your other friends. *Gracias,* but I'll choose my own husband—that is, if I decide to marry."

"Tere, you are a most willful child. In my day, a young woman married the man her *papá* chose, and was happy about it. I don't understand why I have been cursed with such stubborn daughters."

Teresa rose on tiptoes and kissed her father's nose. "Because, Papá, you are a most stubborn man."

The scowl on the man's face disappeared, but his deep-blue eyes held their fiery sparkle. "If I did not love you so much, Teresita, I would have written you out of my will long ago." Then his gaze met Allison's, and the scowl returned. His eyes narrowed, turning a cold steel blue. "What is *she* doing here?"

"Becky Lee brought by the new dress she made me." Teresa twirled to show it off. "You like it?"

"*Sí, sí,* but if she's done, send her on her way." The man lowered his voice, but Allison could still hear him. "Know your place, Teresa. You know how I feel about your keeping company with servants."

"She is not a servant, Papá," Teresa whispered harshly. "And I keep company with whomever I please. You will not do to me what you did to Isa."

The man flinched as though he had been slapped.

Instantly, Teresa's face softened. "I'm sorry, Papá. I do not mean to hurt you. But, please, please allow me to make my own decisions. I have a brain, and I have a heart. The two do not work independently, no matter what you mandate."

The man gave his daughter a sad smile and kissed her

forehead, holding her close for a few seconds. Then he turned and strode from the room.

Allison stood at the entrance to the Cardona Pomales estate wondering what to do next. Before her and to her left and right lay acres and acres of grapevines. Behind her was the hacienda-style mansion she'd just left. Apparently, the Cardona Pomales family had made its fortune in vineyards.

She didn't want to go back to the Thompson cabin. That Thompson woman was horrid and abusive. She didn't know how to get to the cabin, anyway.

She also had no idea where the nearest town was. Even if she knew, what could she do in a town with no money? Maybe she could camp out in the woods. She loved camping. She was planning to be a forest ranger, wasn't she? But although she'd taken survival training last summer, she'd never really been on her own. How long could she last without food and shelter?

What year was it, anyway? It might help if she at least knew the year. She hadn't spotted any calendars at the estate, but she did notice electric lights, though no televisions or telephones were in view. When was electricity discovered? Allison vaguely remembered the discovery being in the late 1800s. So this would place her in the late 1800s or the early 1900s. From what Allison had seen of Teresa's clothes, it could be either.

Frustrated, Allison began to walk down the dirt road toward some trees in the distance. As she walked, she couldn't help wondering where Becky had headed after leaving the estate that day. Was Allison supposed to go there? Becky was making Allison relive her past to help her. Help her do what? Did helping her mean Allison had to do everything Becky did, exactly? How could Allison help Becky when she didn't share Becky's memories and had no way of contacting the girl while she was stuck in her body?

Allison made up her mind. As long as she didn't know what she was supposed to do for Becky, she'd try to survive by making her own choices, regardless of whether they were the choices Becky would have made. But a thought crossed Allison's mind that made her shudder. If she didn't figure out what Becky needed and helped her get it, Allison might never return to her own life in the future.

CHAPTER 6

Allison found it odd how quickly she had adjusted to another person's body. It was as easy as getting used to a new set of clothes. Only two things had felt a bit strange. The first was Becky's height. Allison was almost five feet, six inches tall; Becky seemed to be at least six inches shorter. Six inches made quite a difference on your perspective of the world, especially an unfamiliar world such as this one.

The other difference was that Allison was right-handed. She had a very strong feeling that Becky was a lefty. Allison kept wanting to step out with her right foot, but her left seemed to be fighting her. And her right arm seemed awkward, clumsy.

After half an hour of walking down the dirt road, she forgot she was not in her own body. She was only aware of the unfamiliar surroundings.

The day was horribly hot. By the time Allison reached the edge of the forest, her right arm and shoulder were throbbing, and she was sweaty and thirsty. *Now what?* she thought. Maybe she should turn off her mind and let her legs lead the way. If only that were possible.

Allison stayed on the dirt road, searching for something—anything—that might feel or appear familiar. Soon she came to a well-worn path that led into the woods. She stared at the spot where the path disappeared under the trees. Exhaling slowly, she stepped onto the path and followed it into the forest.

The temperature seemed to drop at least ten degrees in the heavy shade of the dense woods. Allison filled her lungs with the fresh, cool air. She loved the moist, earthy smell of woods. Funny how time seemed to stand still in a forest. Out there, where civilization flourished, the year could be 1620 or 2060, but you'd never know by looking at areas untouched by humans.

She followed the path until she came to a fork. The path to her left was well-worn like the path she was on. The path to her right was less traveled. Something made her want to stay on a less-traveled path. She turned right and continued.

Allison followed the quickly disappearing path until, at last, it vanished into the brush and ferns. Well, so much for the road less traveled. She wanted to venture farther, but she didn't want to risk getting lost. Allison thought back to her survival training: *Mark the route you follow.*

Perhaps she could use a sharp stone to mark an X in tree trunks. With her bare foot, she pushed aside clumps of brush, searching for sharp stones. Something cold slithered over her foot.

She jumped and bit her lip to stifle a scream that was halfway out her throat. A thin garter snake darted away from her and disappeared under a thick clump of ferns. Allison shuddered. Maybe walking through the forest wasn't such a good idea, especially barefooted.

As she was about to return to the main road, something

seemed to pull her like a magnet toward the heart of the forest. "Okay, okay," she muttered, "I'll keep going... for a little while, anyway."

Before she moved on, she found a couple of angular rocks to mark the trees, and a fallen branch that would make a good walking stick. Allison used the stick to push aside tall grasses and warn anything living under them to scamper or slither away from her approaching bare feet. She made slow but steady progress, looking back on occasion to check her marks.

Once more, the thought crossed her mind that this was a crazy thing to do. What was she accomplishing? How could she possibly live in a forest without even a knife? Another problem was her clothing. How cold did it get in these woods at night? And how could she survive without a jacket or coat? No, this was definitely crazy.

Allison was about to turn back for the second time, when she heard it: running water. The sound was coming from the direction she was facing. She hurried on.

The farther she went, the louder became the sound of rushing water. The ground felt softer and more moist, and the vegetation seemed greener, more lush. A strong breeze rustled the leaves and tickled her hair.

A green path of velvety moss led her to the edge of a shallow creek. Smooth rocks in the stream piled like steps over which miniature waterfalls tumbled, carrying swirling bits of grass, leaves, and twigs. The water was so clear that Allison could make out every pebble and grain of sand that carpeted the creek's bottom.

With a tiny squeak of pleasure, Allison stepped onto the squishy ground that banked the creek. It was an easy step from the bank to the water.

She dipped a toe into the water and jerked back, shocked by the sudden iciness. It was almost as cold as freshly melted snow. Delighted, Allison stuck her whole foot into the water until she felt bottom, held her breath, and eased in the other foot. Soon her legs were numb up to the waterline, which only reached midcalf. She cupped her hands in the water and sipped the fresh, icy liquid, quenching her thirst.

Noticing that the hem of her dress was getting wet, she wrung it out, twisted it into a knot in front of her, and tucked it under her waistband. That left her long, drooping bloomers dipping into the creek. Annoyed with her impractical attire, Allison yanked up the legs of the bloomers to the tops of her thighs and retied the frayed blue ribbon.

The magnetic pull she had felt earlier seemed to tug her up the creek. She balanced on smooth rocks and stones that formed natural steps up the miniature rapids. Although small, the swirling rapids were forceful, and Allison had to be careful not to lose her balance. Whenever possible, she walked on the more solid sandy bottom, dragging her feet in the sand and pebbles, enjoying the sensation.

The sun was still high in the sky, which meant it was around noon or early afternoon. If she didn't stumble on to something soon, she'd go back to the Cardona Pomales estate and beg Teresa for help.

The stream meandered through the forest. Sometimes it narrowed under a long canopy of overhanging, interlocking branches, other times it widened, pushing the trees apart and revealing the robin's-egg blue sky and brilliant sunshine. Soon the creek widened and dead-ended a few hundred yards ahead. Tall pines clustered on the edges of the widened stream and provided deep shade. A huge rock formation stood at the end, over which a tall, thin waterfall cascaded to the pool below. The spot looked appealing.

Allison quickened her pace, eager to rest at the foot of the waterfall. As she drew nearer, the crash of water plunging to the pool and rocks below filled her ears. It surprised her how thunderous falling water could sound. Reminded of thunder, her mind drifted back to the hospital room and to Becky. What did the girl want of her, and how long would it take to find out?

Pushing away her thoughts, she found she had reached the pool's edge. The pool formed an almost perfect circle, with the waterfall on one end and the creek at the opposite end. Huge boulders, spaced around the pool and bordered by lush ferns, formed natural resting spots on which to sit and dip one's feet.

And that was precisely what someone was doing. On one smooth, flat boulder at the edge of the water sat a boy staring straight ahead while his feet and fishing line dangled in the water. He apparently had not noticed Allison approaching.

Could it be? Allison squinted and moved in closer to get a better look. It was!

Allison was so surprised to see another human being in this wilderness, and someone she knew, no less, that she spoke without thinking:

"Joshua?"

CHAPTER 7

Joshua didn't move. Allison realized he couldn't hear her over the sound of the crashing waterfall. She stood in the middle of the stream, gentle swirls of cold water spinning around her legs, and stared at the boy. Slowly, as though mesmerized, he lifted his head and turned toward her. When their eyes met, his face lit up like a sunrise. Allison couldn't help but smile back.

They remained as still as the trees surrounding them, smiling and staring into each other's eyes across the width of the pool. A feeling of warmth and deep tranquillity spread through her: a sense of being at home despite a strange and distant time and place, as if the eyes of this boy were the eyes of an old friend, someone she'd known forever. But all at once, Allison realized she was staring at him...and he at her...and she began to feel self-conscious.

Why am I feeling this way about a boy I've only met once? she wondered.

At the same moment, Joshua's gaze left her face and traveled down to her exposed legs. He quickly looked away, seemingly embarrassed, and began fussing with his fishing pole.

Allison looked down. The skirt of the faded calico dress was twisted into a knot and tucked under the waistband, fully exposing the bloomers that were rolled up to the tops of her thighs.

Oops! she thought. *This wouldn't look too great in my own time—what must it look like in 18-whatever? Bloomers are underwear, for goodness sakes. I'm showing my underwear to a boy I've just met!*

The self-consciousness was replaced by giggles. Allison was used to showing a lot of her legs—in miniskirts, shorts, bikinis. And although she wasn't used to being seen in her underwear, bloomers were so baggy, they didn't feel like underwear. The image of standing, exposed from the top of her bloomers down, in front of a boy who had probably never seen a woman's knee, was hilarious. No wonder he turned away.

The more Allison giggled, the more flustered Joshua seemed to get. Suddenly, Allison lost her balance and splashed backward into the creek.

"Oh!" she cried, sitting on the sandy bottom, legs sprawled before her as twigs and leaves swirled by. "I'm drenched!"

In a flash, Joshua was behind her, yanking her up by the armpits. "You all right, Becky?" he said, turning her to look at him.

"Do I look all right? I'm soaking, and I've nothing to change into."

Allison squeezed her dripping braids and looked up at Joshua. There was that annoying impish grin, spreading from ear to ear. His eyes danced as though he wanted to burst out laughing. Then he did.

"It's not funny!" Allison shoved him away and began wading for shore. Her skirt had come loose and was dragging in the water, making it hard to walk. In a huff, she grabbed the long skirt and yanked it up, high out of the water. "Cover your eyes, or you might see something you don't want to."

Joshua roared. Allison could hear him splashing behind her as he tried to follow. "C'mon, Becky, don't be mad. It's just that—"

"That what?" Allison spun around, her eyes flashing like fireworks. "I look like a wet hen or a drowned rat?"

"Oh, no, ma'am!" Joshua swallowed a smile, but his eyes were still laughing. "State you're in, I wouldn't dare say anything like that."

"What's that supposed to mean?"

"Nothin', Becky, really." Joshua stared at Allison's face for a second. "You really are riled up, aren't you?"

Allison's eyes narrowed. "One more comment about my state of mind, and I'll—I'll—"

Joshua tilted back his head and howled.

"I warned you!" Allison thrust her hands against the boy's chest, propelling him backward into the stream. Arms and legs splashed and slapped the water.

"Oww!" He sat up and shook his head like a bushy dog trying to dry off. "No fair! I didn't push you in."

Allison grinned at the sight. "Maybe not physically, but if you hadn't made me laugh..."

"I made you laugh?" Then Joshua got a look on his

face that told Allison he knew just why she'd laughed. He tried to stand up, but the current pushed him back down. "C'mon, Becky Lee. Give me a hand."

"Okay, fair's fair. You helped me up." Still conscious of her bruised arm, Allison offered Joshua her left hand.

The boy grabbed her hand and pulled her down beside him into the cold, clear water.

"Ohh! I'll get you for this!" But Allison was giggling again, her anger washed away by the current.

She sat up on her knees and splashed Joshua. He splashed her back. For the next ten minutes, they sat in waist-high, ice-cold water splashing each other like a couple of toddlers in a wading pool.

Shivering and laughing, they helped each other up and threw themselves, panting, onto the bank of the creek. The sun was warm, but not enough to melt the chill from their bones or to dry their clothes.

Joshua sat up. "Help me make a fire, Becky. We'll never dry off this way."

Allison pushed herself up onto her elbows. "You've got something to start a fire with?"

Joshua gave her a strange look. "Course I do. You know that." He shook his head. "You get some wood. I'll fix up the rocks."

Still shivering, Allison poked around under the trees, gathering an armful of dry branches, then deposited the wood next to Joshua. He had already started a small smoldering fire, near the spot where he had been fishing, and was adding bits of dry leaves and pine needles. Beside him sat a basket of fish.

"Fish!" Allison collapsed next to him. "I'm starving!"

"Figured we'd kill two birds with one stone—eat and get warm and dry."

Allison looked around uncomfortably. Seeming to sense something, Joshua asked, "Something wrong?"

"Mmm, it's just that . . . well, these clothes are going to take forever to dry if we keep them on, and . . ."

Joshua snorted. "Now who's bashful?"

Again without thinking, Allison laughed and said, "I hardly know you. I'm not undressing in front of a boy I've just met. Even if I—" The look on Joshua's face made her stop midsentence. "I mean, I can't—"

"Hardly know me? Becky Lee, what's gotten into you? We've known each other since we was babies."

"Well, sure we have, it's just that— Well, you've never seen me . . . ?"

"Seen you what?" Joshua looked into Allison's eyes, and she turned away, blushing. "No, of course not! It ain't proper. I wasn't suggesting we walk around neck-ed. Look!"

Joshua ran to the waterfall and vanished behind it. A few seconds later, he returned carrying two rolled-up blankets.

"Blankets! Wow, where'd you—?" Allison stopped before she made yet another blunder. "I mean, this is great. We can get undressed and wrap up in blankets."

"And eat." Joshua drew a knife from his pocket. "Go into the trees and get undressed while I gut the fish. I'll get them roasting."

By the time Allison returned, wearing the blanket like a sarong wrapped under her armpits and carrying her wet clothes, Joshua had already spread out his clothes to dry.

His blanket was wrapped around his waist like a skirt, and he was kneeling in front of the fire, hanging the gutted fish on thin green branches above the flames. He had propped open the sides of the fish with short sticks.

Feeling self-conscious again, Allison tiptoed to the fire and spread out the calico dress, bloomers, and camisole on soft pine needles. When she was done, she knelt in front of Joshua.

"Anything I can do?"

"No, I'm just about done," he said, hanging the fourth fish on a branch above the fire and poking the other end of the stick into the ground. "Just settle in. The fish don't take but a few—" Joshua looked up and his eyes opened wide. He stared at Allison's bruised shoulder and arm. "Becky Lee, what on Earth?"

He was at her side in an instant. "It was *her,* wasn't it?" Joshua examined the bruised arm. His touch was butterfly soft. When he looked back up, his eyes had lost their laughter.

"Wasn't it?" he insisted.

Allison shrugged her good shoulder. "I'm not sure...I guess so."

"What do you mean, you're not sure? You couldn't have slept through a beating like this."

"I just don't know." Allison turned away. How could she explain?

Joshua's eyes narrowed. "You been having any more of them spells you was telling me about?"

"Spells?"

"You don't have to be afraid to tell me, Becky. Anyway, I know it was your mama. It's always your mama."

Joshua continued to stare at her arm as if the mere act of looking could mend it. "Can you lift it?"

Allison lifted the arm and winced. "But it's not as bad as it was this morning. I doubt it's sprained. Just bruised."

"I swear, Becky Lee"—Joshua's voice quivered—"if Sadie Thompson hurts you once more, I'll kill her. I swear I will."

Allison shivered. "Don't say that! Anyway, she'll never have another chance to touch me."

"Now what are you talking about? Why won't she?"

"Because"—Allison turned and looked into Joshua's eyes—"I'm never going back there, that's why."

CHAPTER 8

Allison leaned against a boulder and licked her greasy fingers. "That had to be the best fish I've ever eaten."

Joshua chuckled. "You always say that."

"Oh... I guess I would—I mean do—I guess I do."

Joshua gave her a strange look and shook his head. "You were late again, today. Didn't think you'd make it."

"You were waiting for me?" *So I did do what Becky was supposed to do.*

"We always meet here Tuesday afternoons."

"Oh, sure—of course, we do."

Joshua gave her that look again. "All right, Becky Lee. Something mighty peculiar's going on."

What am I going to do now? Can I trust him? No, he'll think I'm crazy, and he's my only friend. I've got to fake it.

"There is? I don't know what you mean."

"The way you're acting, the things you say. Why, even the way you talk is strange. If I didn't know you so well, I'd believe you was a completely different person."

Allison turned her back to him and busied herself with shifting their clothes around to get them dry. "Well, that's just plain silly," she said, trying to imitate Joshua's manner of speech.

"I'd think it was, too, if I hadn't been watching you for the last couple of hours."

"Tell me what you mean, Joshua." Allison tried to sound interested but not too interested. She leaned against the boulder.

"It's—it's everything. The way you walk, the way you hold your head. The fire in your eyes. I've never seen you so...so..."

"So what? Tell me, please."

"So bold, so spunky, so sure of yourself."

"I'm the same old Becky Lee. See—my calico dress, my braids, my bruised arm. I'm all here."

Joshua shook his head. "I know, I know. It don't make sense. But *something*'s different. The Becky Lee Thompson I've always known would never wander up the creek with her bloomers showing. She's shy, soft-spoken, keeps her eyes and head down like a whipped puppy. Sometimes her eyes hold such pain, it 'bout breaks my heart to look in them. When she laughs, she puts her hands in front of her face as if it was a crime to be happy—why, she's never whooped it up the way you and I did earlier in the creek. And"—he lowered his voice to a whisper—"she needs to be taken care of."

Joshua turned her toward him and took Allison's face in his hands, gently lifting her chin. "The girl I see today is like a wild mare who'll never really be tamed. She's a spitfire. She's everything I want Becky to be. That's why I was laughing over there in the creek—I was so happy. I saw fight in those eyes. It's not that I don't love her the way she is, it's just that she needs to be a fighter to survive. And I want her—need her—to survive. If she doesn't stand up to Sadie Thompson, I'm afraid the woman will kill her—you. See what you've got me doing? I'm acting like you're a whole other person."

Allison slowly released the breath she'd been holding since Joshua touched her face. She'd never been this close to a boy. She had no time to waste on boys. As far as she could see, boys in the nineties only wanted one thing. And she wasn't ready or willing to deal with the pressure of having to fight them off or give in and "put out." It was easier to ignore their existence and concentrate on schoolwork.

But Joshua wasn't like anyone she'd ever met, boy or girl. She felt comfortable with him—even in a blanket sarong. She knew she could trust him not to try to make a move on her the moment she let down her guard. And there was something else. His sincerity and sweetness touched her heart—no, her soul. She felt as though she *had* known him forever. That they had met before, in another lifetime. Was it possible? Could they be soul mates?

"Becky?" Joshua searched Allison's face. "You all right?"

"Mmm, yes. I'm okay—uh, all right."

"It wasn't another spell, was it? You were staring at me."

"Spell? Do I do that often? Have a spell, I mean."

"Don't you remember?"

Allison leaned back and shook her head. She could honestly say she didn't remember.

"I've been with you a few times when you just go into a trance or something. You stare straight ahead for a few minutes, then you come out of it and can't remember anything about it. You told me sometimes you lose hours and don't get your sewing done. You find yourself wandering somewhere and have no idea how you got there. That's when your ma loses her temper."

Blackouts! I've heard of people having blackouts. Maybe Becky's got a brain disorder or maybe it's a psychological thing. With a mother like Sadie, who wouldn't have blackouts?

"Don't you remember, Becky?"

I hate lying to him. Anyway, I can't fake it much longer, Joshua's too bright. He's almost figured it out already. Almost. But will he believe me? I have to trust him—I need someone to confide in if I'm going to survive.

"Joshua, I have to tell you—" Allison gasped and jumped up. "Something grabbed my hair!"

She turned to look at what it might have been. From behind the boulder poked a black nose. Slowly a dark gray head emerged, revealing a black mask and two shiny black eyes. Two delicate black claws came up to the eyes and covered them.

Joshua roared with laughter. "Well, one thing sure hasn't changed," he managed between chortles. "You're still skittish about animals."

"Stop it! Stop laughing at me." Allison punched Joshua's shoulder, but it only made him laugh harder. "I am *not* skittish about animals. I just didn't expect a raccoon to walk right up and—" Allison caught Joshua's laughter and couldn't finish.

In the meantime, the little raccoon scuttled around the boulder and plopped down next to Joshua, raising his front claws in begging position.

"Oh, my gosh," cried Allison with delight. "Is he tame?"

"Of course, he's tame. This is Bubba." Joshua rubbed Bubba's ears. "He just wants a handout, don't you, boy? Grab the fish heads, Becky. There's still some meat on those."

Allison handed a fish head to the little raccoon. He took it in his tiny claws, dragged it to the water in his mouth, and washed it in a busy, fastidious manner before beginning to nibble it.

"He's so cute! I love raccoons."

"Since when?" Joshua said in a tone that implied that he thought Becky was afraid of anything that moved.

"Uh," Allison began, trying to think quickly, "since now. Who can resist that face? How'd you ever tame him?" she asked, deliberately changing the subject from her back to Bubba.

"I found his mama lying dead in the woods a ways down, and next to her, 'most starved to death, was this tiny baby coon. Never told you 'bout him 'cuz of the way you felt 'bout animals. But I nursed him back to life, with Magda's help, and, hey"—Joshua leaped up and started gathering their clothes—"I almost forgot about Magda! Hurry up, Becky. Let's get dressed. The clothes are dry. We can take Bubba home and get your arm looked at, all at the same time."

"Magda?" Allison took the clothes Joshua handed her.

"Sure, she can use some of her special liniment on your

arm. And it's been ages since she's seen you. We never seem to have much time to do things anymore. Ever since your ma started making you sew most every day and night. So hurry up and get dressed."

Allison took shelter under the trees and changed. The light cotton camisole and bloomers were dry, but the calico dress was still damp.

When Allison returned, Joshua was dressed and had already doused the fire. As Allison handed him his blanket, she remembered something. *How does he store the blankets behind the waterfall?* she wondered. She was tempted to ask but was afraid it would raise more questions about her identity. Although she wanted to tell Joshua who she really was, she wanted to meet this Magda first.

Joshua took the blankets and headed for the waterfall. She ran after him. "May I come?"

"Sure. I know how you like sitting behind the waterfall. We don't have a lot of time, though."

Allison gasped. She loved sitting behind waterfalls, but it took her a moment to figure out how he knew that. She had forgotten that Joshua thought he was talking to Becky.

"I won't take long, I promise. I love watching the world through a shivering sheet of water. And the sound of the falls crashing around me, it's—I don't know..."

Joshua grinned. "I know what you mean. That's why I come here so much."

He led Allison to a natural path that ran along the craggy rock formation and behind the stream of falling water. Hidden by the waterfall was a small cave.

So that was it. Joshua had a secret hideaway, stocked with candles, blankets, food. He could live like a hermit here . . . for all Allison knew, he did.

Allison turned to face the waterfall. Delighted, she thrust her hands into the cascade of water. "It's like a tiny paradise, with the fishing hole and the waterfall. I could stay here forever."

The moment she heard her own words, Allison bit her lip. The words sent a shiver down her spine. She jerked her hands from the cascade and rubbed them along her arms. She couldn't believe what she'd said. What if the Powers That Be heard her? She was terrified that that was exactly what might happen. Much as she enjoyed this place and being with Joshua, she had to go home.

"Becky?"

"Mmm?" Allison turned. Joshua had tucked the blankets in the cave and was waiting for her. She smiled. "I'm ready."

Joshua led the way past the waterfall, along the rock path, and into the woods. Suddenly, he stopped. "Where's Bubba? Bubba! C'mon, boy."

The bushes behind them rustled, and a round, gray body waving a striped gray-and-white tail toppled onto the path, sat up, and scrambled off, leading the way through the trees.

Laughing, Joshua grabbed Allison's hand and pulled her after him, trying to keep up with the little raccoon. Finally, Bubba vanished under a clump of ferns, and Joshua slowed down.

"He's gone again," Allison said.

Joshua shrugged. "He'll be back when he's ready. He knows we're going to Magda's."

Although they'd stopped running, Joshua continued to hold Allison's hand. Their hands fitted perfectly, interlocking like two matching pieces of a jigsaw puzzle. It felt nice, right. His hand was warm, and the warmth seemed to seep through her skin and into her bloodstream, straight to her heart. Would she ever be able to experience this again? If she woke from her coma, would she ever share a deep, comfortable silence like this while holding hands with a boy? Just walking in the forest—enjoying the trees; the moist, earthy smells; the cool breeze—with no need to speak, because sharing the silence was more powerful than anything they could say.

"Becky," Joshua said in a whisper so soft it barely broke the silence, "look."

He had frozen in midstep, staring straight ahead. Allison followed his gaze. Beneath two tall pines, in a slanting ray of afternoon sun that splintered the branches, stood a doe and her fawn. Mother and child seemed locked in time, their brown bodies blending with the tree trunks and dry pine needles, providing perfect camouflage.

Allison held her breath. Her mother always said, "Seeing a deer in the forest is the closest thing to heaven on Earth." She couldn't agree more as she looked into the dark, limpid eyes of the mother deer.

Joshua squeezed her hand. She looked up into his ever-smiling face, and a silent understanding passed between them. She knew he felt exactly as she did at that moment. Allison was also aware that a new bond had been formed—a bond between Joshua and *Allison*.

CHAPTER 9

Bubba returned a few times while Allison and Joshua meandered through the forest. The little raccoon would glare at them for a moment, scurry ahead, stop, and look back, as if to say "Hurry up, slowpokes. What're you waiting for?" Then, impatiently, he'd scamper on and vanish in the underbrush.

At last, they came to a small clearing beneath the pines, at the edge of which a tiny cottage huddled in deep shade. The front yard was swept clean of pine needles, exposing moist ground spotted with crazy-quilt patches of thick moss. Gem-colored primroses bordered the sides of the cottage, and low ferns guarded the front door like stubby sentries.

Bubba scrambled across the yard. When he reached the cottage door, he scraped the wood with his front claws. Allison and Joshua watched from the edge of the clearing as the door opened and the raccoon scuttled inside. A woman stepped into the doorway, her face hidden by the shadow of the eaves.

"I have prepared sarsaparilla tea," she called out, "and stew. Come." She turned, leaving the door open, and disappeared inside.

Allison turned to Joshua. "Was she speaking to us?"

"Yep." Joshua led Allison by the hand. "Best not keep her waiting. Magda's not partial to being kept waiting."

"How'd she know we were out here?" Allison ran to keep up with him.

"Magda knows lots of things."

They stepped through the doorway into a cool, dark room full of exotic fragrances. Allison first recognized the strong scents of lavender, rose, and lilac. Then the more subtle aroma of cooking herbs and other strange, foreign smells tickled her senses. When her eyes adjusted to the darkness, she could see that most of the smells were coming from dried bunches of flowers, herbs, leafy branches, and gnarled roots hanging upside down from the rough-beamed ceiling.

The cottage was made up of one small room divided by a curtain at one end. A crude table took up most of the middle of the room. The walls were covered with shelves and hanging cabinets that held dozens of bottles, vials, and tiny cheesecloth bags stuffed to bursting. At the wall opposite the front door, Magda knelt in front of a stone fireplace, lifting the teakettle from the fire.

"Sit, sit." Magda turned and shook raven-black hair from her face—the most incredible face Allison had ever seen. Magda reminded her of an exquisite doll Allison had once admired at an antique shop: a milky complexion in contrast to her dark hair, the perfect features of an ancient Greek sculpture, and alert blue eyes that adorned her face like jewels. But Magda's most striking quality was the serene expression of someone who is at peace with herself and her surroundings.

Magda rose and moved toward them, seeming to stumble, but when she took the next step, Allison noticed the woman had a severe limp. It was impossible to tell whether Magda's limp was due to a deformed leg or one that was significantly shorter than the other because her legs were hidden beneath a heavy burgundy-colored skirt that swept the floorboards as she walked. Magda poured the steaming brown liquid into earthenware cups.

"Are you hungry, *muchachos*?" Like Teresa Cardona Pomales, Magda spoke with a delicate Spanish accent.

Joshua stretched and patted his belly, winking at Magda. "You know me, Magda, I'm always hungry."

"Becky?" Magda turned her intense eyes to Allison.

"It's strange, it feels like hours since we ate, but I'm not very hungry."

"Not strange at all," said Joshua, taking a sip of tea. "You always eat like a sparrow."

"Finish your tea, and I will serve you both some stew. You need not eat very much if you do not wish to, Becky."

"She'll eat," Joshua said. "She needs some meat on her bones." He attempted a frown, but his laughing eyes and the grin that seemed to always play with the corners of his mouth ruined the effect.

Allison was about to protest, disliking anyone to order her about, but she realized that Joshua meant well and was really thinking of her as Becky, so she decided to keep quiet. *It's what Becky would have done.* Instead, she took a sip of tea. Not bad. She'd never tasted sarsaparilla. It tasted a bit like flat Dr. Pepper, her favorite soft drink.

"Before we eat, Magda," said Joshua, "could you take a look at Becky's arm? I thought you might use some of your special liniment on it."

"She hurt her arm?" Magda sat next to Allison.

"Something like that," Joshua muttered.

"May I see, Becky?"

Allison pushed up her sleeve. Magda's placid expression remained unchanged while she gently lifted the girl's arm. But as she held the arm in her hands, examining the bruises, the woman's face suddenly contorted with pain. She cried out and turned away.

Alarmed, Allison pulled back her arm. "Are you all right, Magda?"

Magda doubled over and swayed back and forth, moaning as if in a trance. Joshua leaped to her side and knelt beside her, his face full of concern.

"Magda?" he said softly.

When she didn't respond, Allison said, "Joshua, shouldn't we do something? What's wrong with her?"

"We can't touch her. We have to wait for it to pass."

"Wait for what to pass? What's happening to her, Joshua? She seems in horrible pain."

Magda's moaning and writhing lessened, and she began to sit up.

"Magda, are you back?" Joshua whispered.

"*Sí*, Joshua, I'm here," she said between deep breaths.

Joshua placed his hand on her shoulder. "Did you see something?"

"*Un momento*—give me a moment." Magda covered

her face with her hands and took another deep breath. When she removed her hands, Magda turned to Allison. "I see a large woman moving toward a girl. Reaching for her, grabbing her, pulling her hair and arms. The girl struggles; the woman wrenches her arm behind her and twists. The girl screams. I feel her pain, her terror. I recognize the girl's face, her body. It is this face, this body."

Magda touched Allison's face with her fingertips. She looked down at the bruised arm, then moved her gaze slowly back to Allison's face. In a hushed voice, she said, "But the girl who screamed was not you. You are *la otra*...the other."

Magda led Allison to her bedroom, the space behind the curtain, and helped Allison remove her dress so Magda could apply liniment to the bruised shoulder and upper arm. The liniment was cool and soothing and smelled of camphor, eucalyptus, and wintergreen. And Magda's touch itself felt warm and healing.

Allison glanced around the tiny enclosure. It held a small cot, above which hung a large, elaborately sculpted silver crucifix. The remaining space was taken up by a homemade shrine. A wooden prie-dieu stood before the modest altar. The narrow kneeling bench had a prayer shelf at the top, on which lay a worn leather prayer book and an ancient Bible, its pages warped and its corners dog-eared from years of handling.

The altar was covered with white linen embroidered in gold thread. On it stood a delicately carved and painted statue of the Virgin Mary surrounded by several statuettes of saints. Votive candles burned in red and blue glass tumblers. A crystal-beaded rosary lay at the foot of the Virgin.

When they were done, Magda led Allison back to the kitchen table. The moment he saw them, Joshua flew up from his chair, toppling it backward. "I can't stand it anymore. Will one of you tell me what's going on?"

"*Siéntate,* Joshua," said Magda, "*y ten paciencia.*"

"All right, I'll sit," he replied, standing his chair upright. "But I won't be patient."

Magda set an earthenware bowl in front of Allison, then another in front of Joshua. "The stiffness should be gone by morning, and the soreness soon after," she said to Allison.

"Magda, please," Joshua insisted.

Magda sighed. "I cannot tell you any more than I have, Joshua. The rest is up to Becky."

Allison stared into the empty brown bowl. Bits of iridescent enamel gleamed in the dim light of the kerosene lamp. She bit her lip as she thought of what to say.

"I'm not from here. I was born in 1982, and—"

Joshua gave a short, nervous laugh. "You mean 1892, right Becky? You're fourteen, and you were born in 1892."

"I *am* fourteen years old, but I was born in 1982." Allison glanced sideways at Joshua. "And my name is Allison Anne Blair."

Joshua's face turned pale. He looked as though he had eaten a piece of bad meat and needed to throw up. Allison looked at Magda. Her face was as calm as a clear lake on a windless day.

"I was in an accident a few days ago, I think—I mean

in 1996. I fell down a ravine and hit my head. A girl found me and got help. I was taken to a hospital in a coma—unconscious. The girl who helped me was Becky Lee Thompson. She took over my body and sent me back in hers to help her. But I don't know what she wants me to do."

Joshua sat with his head in his hands, shaking it back and forth. "This can't be true. Becky, maybe you're just having one of your spells..."

"Allison—my name is Allison. I know it sounds crazy, Joshua. How do you think I feel?" Allison reached over and placed her hand on Joshua's. She had to make him believe her.

Joshua stiffened at her touch. "It sounds worse than crazy, girl. What you're saying is that Becky Lee is possessed by the ghost of a girl that's not even been born yet."

Allison gave him a wry grin. "I think you have to be dead to be a ghost. I don't think I'm dead yet."

Joshua shook his head again. "This is nothing to joke about. The only thing that's making me listen to this crazy talk is that I don't even know you anymore. You aren't anything like my Becky."

Allison thought for a moment. "What's the date? Maybe I can prove to you I'm from the future."

"April 17, 1906," Joshua said in a resigned voice.

Allison gasped. "April... 1906? Are we still in northern California? Near San Francisco?"

"About seventy-five miles northeast of San Francisco."

"Well," said Allison, "it's close, but maybe not close enough. A day or two from now, the eighteenth or the nineteenth—I can't remember exactly—there's going to be a horrible earthquake in San Francisco. What isn't destroyed by the quake will be burned by fires. But I don't know how much we'll feel up here. Anyway, that's still at least a day away, and I need you to believe me now."

"I already told you I know you're different. It's this girl-from-the-future thing, and inside my Becky, no less! It—it makes my head hurt." He groaned and covered his head with his arms.

Allison thought about the movie *Aliens* and all the other science fiction and horror movies she'd seen in which an alien *thing* was living inside a perfectly normal-looking human being. The last thing she wanted was for Joshua to be repulsed by her, to think she was a freak or a grotesque creature of some sort.

"Joshua," she whispered, "please don't be afraid of me. I'm still a person. I'm not a ghost or a changeling or a ghoul. I'm the same person you laughed and played with in the creek and who held your hand in the woods. I'm just not Becky." When Joshua still didn't reply, Allison added, "But I do need your help."

Joshua was silent for a moment. Then he lifted his head and looked up at Allison. His eyes studied her face. The tiniest grin began to wiggle the corners of his mouth. The intense look in his eyes relaxed.

"If there's something I can't turn my back on, it's a person in distress—'specially a lady."

"Magda," said Allison as she finished the last of her stew, "you said I was 'the other.' How did you know that?"

"I sensed it. You did not seem to have knowledge of

the terror, of how you got the bruises. The vision came to me from touching your body, just as a vision might come to me from touching something that belonged to someone who had experienced violence. It was as though your body were a foreign object, not a part of you. I did not feel your emotions. I felt the body's energy."

"But that still doesn't explain your choice of words—you said '*la otra*—the other.' "

"I have been expecting you. The last time I saw Becky, I had a . . . *presentimiento* . . ."

"Premonition," Joshua said.

"*Sí,* a premonition. I sensed her future held danger, but I did not know how or when it would happen. So I did not say anything to Becky. I did not wish to frighten her. The words came to me: 'The other shall be here soon.' That is all I know."

Allison shivered at the thought that someone could sense the future. "Have you always been"—she searched for the right word—"psychic?"

Magda brushed strands of long black hair away from her face with slender fingers and nodded. "Ever since I was a child. My brother used to call it *un don*—a gift. My mother called it a curse. Sometimes I agree with her. But it is as much a part of me as my arms and my legs. I would not wish away any of them. One takes the good with the bad."

Allison thought of Magda's severe limp. It was obviously hard on her, but because Magda didn't let it interfere with the day-to-day things she wanted to accomplish, it was not completely disabling. Allison wondered if that was one of the bad things Magda was referring to. Magda's beauty surely must be one of the good things.

"Do you live here alone?" Allison asked Magda.

Joshua laughed. "Why, Magda's never alone. She has dozens of friends in the forest."

As if on cue, Bubba awoke from his nap in the corner and scurried to Magda's side. He sat up in begging position, then scampered to the door to be let out.

They laughed as they watched the little raccoon stand on his hind legs and scratch at the door.

"I'll open it," Joshua offered. When he returned to his chair, Joshua continued. "In winter, Magda lets me sleep in front of the fireplace."

Allison's brow furrowed. "Where do you live the rest of the time?"

"In the waterfall cave," he said. Noticing the puzzled look on Allison's face, he added, "Magda took me in when my parents were killed. I was just a little tyke. Right, Magda?"

She smiled and nodded.

"Miz Teresa brought me to her. But a couple of years ago, I decided to be on my own, so I moved into the cave. I'm almost a full-grown man, you know. I got a job at the Cardona Pomales estate, helping with the vineyards and doing odd jobs. And I look in on Magda a couple of times a week, when I'm not staying here."

"But what about school?"

"Miz Teresa teaches school on the estate. I read and write pretty good."

"Joshua is very bright," Magda said in an affectionate tone. "He picked up Spanish very quickly. And he helped me with my English."

"Are you from Mexico, Magda?" Living in the Napa Valley, Allison was used to Mexican immigrants.

"No, my brother and I were born in Spain, as were the Cardona Pomaleses. Don Carlos sent for my father because of his expertise with the grapes. Don Carlos surrounds himself with experts."

Allison noticed an edge to Magda's voice. "Don Carlos?"

"Don Carlos Cardona Pomales, the owner of the biggest vineyard in the Napa Valley." Magda paused and a shadow seemed to cross her face. "A very formidable man, Don Carlos."

"Yes, I remember," said Allison, thinking of Teresa's wild-haired father.

Now it was Joshua's turn to look puzzled. "You've met him—I mean, Becky has, but you?..."

"Allison. The name is Allison. Yes, I met him and Teresa this morning. That's where Becky was when I... appeared." Allison purposely avoided saying, "When I took over her body." The thought still gave her the creeps, so she could imagine how Joshua felt.

"It was very strange, too," she continued. "I got the feeling Don Carlos doesn't like me—I mean Becky. In fact, it was as though he felt contempt for her."

Joshua snorted. "Don't take it personal. He acts as if anyone who isn't Spanish and from a 'good' family is beneath him."

"He's a bigot?"

Joshua smirked. "I wouldn't say it to his face, but that's about the size of it."

"Where is your family now, Magda?" Allison asked. "Did they go back to Spain?"

Magda stared into the fire of the kerosene lamp. Finally, she spoke.

"My father was killed in a fire on the estate. Mamá died soon after from a broken heart. They were childhood sweethearts, and she couldn't go on without him."

"I'm sorry," said Allison. "I shouldn't have intruded."

"You did not know." Magda gazed around her, taking in the cottage walls, almost as if she were in another trance. "Joselito, my brother, built this cottage, and we moved here—to be away from the estate. Don Carlos did not want us around. He did not want José near his older daughter, Isabel. José and Isa were in love, and Isa was my best friend. But a Velásquez was not good enough for his daughter. Don Carlos had plans for Isa to marry a wealthy landowner.

"Isa and José planned to elope. They were going to send for me, and we were to return to Spain. We wanted to get as far away from her father and the estate as possible.

"They did elope and hid out for a few days, but Don Carlos found them and had them brought back. When it became apparent that Isa was with child, Don Carlos sent her to the Carmelitas—"

"The Carmelite nuns," Joshua explained to Allison. "At the convent south of Monterey, right?" he asked Magda.

Magda nodded. "*Sí,* to the convent, to have her baby. He threatened José and forbade him to ever speak to her again. But José adored Isa and would not be parted from her. He always called her La Rubia because of her golden-red hair." Magda paused and smiled sadly, remembering. "A week later, José made plans to break into the convent and take her away. But he disappeared before he reached there. I've never seen or heard from him since."

Magda fingered the tiny gold crucifix that hung around her neck. "Isa's baby was stillborn. The strain of losing her beloved and his baby was too much. *Se volvió loca*—she went... insane. Don Carlos brought her home and keeps her locked in the west wing. But sometimes she escapes. People say they have seen her wandering in the woods at night and, echoing from the west wing, they hear her wailing cries."

CHAPTER 10

Becky..." Joshua winced. "I mean, Allison, it's getting late. You'll have to be getting back to Becky's—"

"I told you, Joshua, I'm not going back there, and I mean it. I don't ever want to see that woman again."

"I never wanted Becky to go back, either. But she kept insisting Sadie would go looking for her, and when she found her she would..."

Allison shuddered at the thought. "So what should I do, go back there and have her knock me senseless again? That's what she did the last time I saw her."

"When was this?"

"I don't really know. For a while, Becky had me bouncing back and forth from her life to mine. One minute I'd be lying in the hospital room, Mom holding my hand, and the next, I'd be in the cabin, or in the woods running for my life, or in the meadow near the cabin." Allison felt the color rise in her face at the memory. "That's when I first met you."

"We met before today?"

Allison gave Joshua a shy smile. "Once, in the meadow.

You ran after me saying I was late and dragged me into the woods after you. Then Becky's mom..."

"That was you? You didn't seem any different. Distracted maybe, but Becky's always distracted."

"Anyway, the last time I was in the cabin, I woke up sitting at an old sewing machine. When I realized where I was, I tried to escape, but that woman caught me. She got pissed off—" At the look of shock on Joshua's face, Allison rephrased. "She got upset because Becky hadn't finished a dress she was working on. Poor Becky had probably been out for a while—one of her spells, maybe—when I dropped in. So she hadn't gotten much work done. Old Sadie hauled back her fist and let me have it. I blacked out, and the next thing I remember was being back in the hospital."

Joshua clenched his fists. "I bet I know when that happened. I saw Becky a couple of weeks ago, and her face was black and blue. She told me she'd tripped and hit her face on a rock. I'll kill that woman, I swear—"

Magda gasped and made the sign of the cross. "*Cállate*, Joshua, don't say such things."

Allison frowned at Joshua. "I already warned him not to carry on about that woman. She's not worth it."

Magda sat next to Allison and took her hands in hers. "Allison, if you do not wish to go back to Sadie, you may stay with me as long as you like. But there are several problems with that plan. First, as Becky feared, Sadie will not rest until she finds you. Second, Becky sent you here for a purpose. We do not know that purpose, and if you stay here, we may not find out until it is too late."

A finger of ice traced its way up Allison's spine. "What do you mean, Magda?"

"I told you I saw danger in Becky's future. I do not know when that danger will strike or where. But Becky must have known when she met you. It must be that danger she wants you to prevent. To do this, I think you must not only live in her body, you must walk in her footsteps. Becky would not have had the courage to run away from her mother."

Allison let out a slow breath. Magda was right. It was what she herself had suspected. If she didn't help Becky by doing what Becky would do, she might never return home.

"I have to go, then." Allison rose from her chair.

"No, wait," said Joshua, grabbing her arm. Allison sat back down. "I don't understand. How could Becky know about some danger that hasn't happened yet? Does she have powers like yours, Magda?"

"I do not think so."

"And another thing I don't understand. How could Becky travel ninety years into the future and leave her body here? And why did she choose you, Allison?"

Allison shrugged. "As far as I know, this could all be a dream—some parts horrible, some parts nice." Allison felt her color rising again. "But if this isn't a dream, the only thing I can think of is that Becky chose me because my spirit is somehow accessible to her while I'm in the coma. But how she can make her spirit or soul or whatever travel to the future, I haven't a clue.

"We have some incredible inventions in the future. You wouldn't believe half of them, Joshua. But time travel is still science fiction—like Jules Verne's novels. And this isn't even science fiction. It's some kind of supernatural, mind-over-matter, hocus-pocus type of thing."

Joshua shook his head. "It just don't make sense. Except for her spells, Becky's always seemed so normal. Sure she's quiet and shy, but considering what she goes through every day, it don't seem unusual."

"I don't know, maybe the spells hold a clue," said Allison. "If she'd only told me what she wanted. All she said was something like 'I helped you, now you help me.' I wish I could communicate with her somehow. But I can't seem to go back on my own."

"How did you go back before?" Magda said.

"I was drawn back. I'm not sure how." Allison thought about this for a moment. "My mom—I'd hear Mom's voice calling me. But the last few times, it was getting harder to hear her. It was as though I was slipping further from her, maybe falling deeper into the coma—I don't know. This last time, I fought to stay, but Becky was stronger. She forced me from my body and sent me through this wind tunnel..."

When Allison looked up, Joshua was staring at her as if she had just told him she swallowed live snakes—whole—for breakfast. She sighed, frustrated.

"I'm not making it up, if that's what you're thinking. I know it sounds bizarre, but I can't help it. That's what happened. The last thing I remember before the wind tunnel is Becky saying, 'Don't worry, Allison. I'll stay here and keep your ticker tickin'. I'll help you, and you'll help me.'"

Joshua nibbled thoughtfully on a fingernail. "So as long as you're here, Becky has to stay in the future."

"Well, I'm sorry you don't have your precious Becky, Joshua," Allison snapped, annoyed that Joshua appeared to be more concerned with Becky's welfare than hers. "I don't like this any more than you do!"

For the first time since they'd arrived at the cottage, Joshua took Allison's hand. "I'm sorry. I didn't mean it like that. I'm just trying to make sense of things, is all. I don't mean to make it harder on you."

"Oh," was all Allison could think to say. She suddenly felt stupid for losing her temper. She had no right to feel jealous of Becky. Becky had been Joshua's girlfriend long before Allison arrived on the scene. But how do you compete with a girl whose body you're wearing, for Pete's sake?

Joshua squeezed Allison's hand and gave her one of his knee-buckling smiles. "I promised I would help you, Allison, and I never break a promise. If you like, I'll take you to Becky's cabin."

When they arrived at the edge of the forest, Joshua stopped. Ahead of them, the poppy-filled meadow stretched for several hundred yards, at the end of which sat the Thompson cabin. In front of the cabin stood a white stallion, saddled and grazing on nearby grass.

"Wait, Bec—Allison." Joshua pulled her back into the shadow of the trees. "Someone's there."

"So what?"

"The Thompsons aren't what you'd call neighborly. People don't just drop by to pass an afternoon. 'Specially people like this."

"What do you mean?"

Before Joshua could answer, the door opened and a tall figure strode out, slamming the door behind him. The wild white hair and arrogant tilt of the head answered Allison's question. The visitor was Don Carlos Cardona Pomales. He grabbed the horse's reins, leaped into the saddle, and galloped off.

"What do you suppose Don Carlos was doing there?" she asked.

Joshua shrugged and led her farther into the trees. "Your guess is as good as mine. But he didn't seem happy with his meeting. Let's wait a bit longer. See if anything else happens."

A few minutes later, the cabin door banged open and a shrill voice pierced the air. "Rebecca Lee! Rebecca Lee, where are you, girl?"

Sadie Thompson marched down the front steps, heading their way. From her voice and the way she was stomping toward them, Allison could tell she was angry.

Very angry.

"Rebecca Lee! Are you out there?"

Allison took a step backward and bumped into Joshua. He put his hands on her shoulders. "You can't go there now," he whispered. "It would be like walking into a stirred-up hornet's nest."

"But...I have to walk in Becky's footsteps, and she would have returned to the cabin."

"No, wait!" Joshua eased Allison farther into the shadows.

Sadie yelled Becky's name once more and glanced around, scanning the surrounding meadow and trees. She waited another moment, then turned and stomped back into the cabin.

"I have to go, Joshua." Allison pulled away from him.

"I can't let you," Joshua said, turning her to face him. "I'm afraid for you."

Allison rubbed her arms, trying to rid herself of a sudden chill. "I'm afraid, too, but what else can I do? Maybe... maybe we could try to think things through some more... before I go."

"Like what?"

Allison thought for a few minutes. "Let's try to figure out what danger could possibly be lurking in Becky's future. Has she ever mentioned anything she's afraid of?"

The moment she said that, Allison realized there was one thing—or person—that Becky was definitely afraid of. The look on Joshua's face told her he was thinking the same thing.

"Her mother!" they said in unison.

Just then, Sadie Thompson stepped out carrying a small white bundle. She glanced around, scanning the meadow once more, before she rushed down the front steps and disappeared into the forest.

"C'mon!" Joshua took Allison's hand and started running. "Let's get out of here before she comes back. We've got to get to Magda's. We'll figure out what to do when you're safe."

CHAPTER 11

Allison spent the night wrapped in a feather-filled comforter on the floor of Magda's cottage. Joshua had left her with Magda and gone back to his waterfall cave. Allison tossed and turned, unable to rid her mind of Becky and her mission. After what seemed like hours, she finally fell into a fitful sleep.

Images from the past few days flickered in and out of her consciousness. She was in the meadow, walking toward the cabin, and Joshua was calling to her. He seemed to be running in place, yelling to her, begging her to stop, but she couldn't keep her legs from moving toward the cabin.

Then she was crashing through trees in the dark, running for her life. Someone was chasing her, breathing hard. Branches were snapping, cracking. She reached a clearing and stopped. For a moment, she looked down. A thin stream of moonlight illuminated the calico dress.

It was smeared with dark stains. She held up her hands. The same stains. They felt sticky. She gagged. Blood. She was covered in blood.

Allison opened her mouth, but no sound came out. Her body convulsed, emitting a silent scream. The sound of labored breathing, the *thump-thump-thump* of heavy feet hitting earth, joined by the crackling of dry leaves and the snapping of breaking twigs filled the darkness. Allison tried to run, but her legs would not move.

As her heart pounded against her ribs and throbbed in her ears, another sound took over. A weeping voice—the voice of a girl, crying, "Help me! Help me, someone. Help! Joshuaa-aaaa!" Then, she was flying through the air, down the cliff of Devil's Drop, and onto the rocks below. Screams pierced her ears, permeated her brain, shot through her senses. She felt as if her whole body would burst from the screams.

Someone grabbed her shoulders. The screams became unbearable. She tried to pull away, but strong arms held and shook her body.

"Allison! Wake up, Allison. *Por favor, niña,* wake up!"

Allison opened her eyes. She was struggling, pushing away the arms, and screaming. They were her screams.

"*Shhhh, shhhhh,* Allison. It is all right. You are safe. *Cálmate. Shh-shh.*"

At the sound of the soothing voice, Allison relaxed. She gazed around the dark room lit only by a few embers in the fireplace.

The arms held her close, comforted her. "You are safe now, Allison. It was only a bad dream, *una pesadilla*. You are safe."

"Where am I?" Allison was still dazed, confused by the dream.

"You are in my cottage, Magda's cottage… in the forest…"

Allison looked up. "Magda? Oh," she said, remembering. "I'm in the past... Becky's past."

"That is right, the past. Go back to sleep now—rest." Magda settled Allison on the comforter and covered her as though she were a child of three, then stroked her forehead and cooed to her in Spanish. *"Shhhh, duérmete."*

As Allison's mind drifted back into darkness, Magda's voice became another voice, whispering, insisting: "It's time, Allison. It's your turn now. I helped you, now you must help me. Go... into the woods... go... I helped you... now you help me..."

When Allison awoke once more, Magda was gone, the embers had died, and the room was shrouded in darkness. The whispers persisted, "Go, Allison. I need you."

As if in a trance, Allison unwrapped herself from the comforter and went to the door.

"Hurry, Allison. It's time."

With the tiniest creak, the door opened and she stepped into the yard. Her way was lit only by a sliver of moonlight and a sprinkling of stars.

"Into the woods, Allison, go."

Like a zombie, Allison lumbered across the yard.

"This way, Allison. Follow the path."

Allison stepped onto the path and into the woods. Her feet seemed to have a life of their own. Her mind was on automatic pilot, listening to the whispers, following the whispers.

"Hurry, Allison, go to Joshua. Hurry. Joshua can help."

At the sound of Joshua's name, Allison's pace quickened. Soon she heard the crash of the waterfall in the distance. The ground felt softer, more moist.

"Hurry, hurry! Joshua can help."

Allison began to run. She believed the voice: Whatever the problem, Joshua could help. When she reached the edge of the forest, she stopped. The waterfall and pool beyond gleamed like mercury in the moonlight. Tall pines surrounding the pool loomed ominously, stretching upward and disappearing in the star-sprinkled blackness.

"Go, Allison. Go to Joshua. Hurry!"

Allison picked her way over the rocky path, behind the waterfall, and to the cave. The thundering water was deafening.

"Joshua!" Allison called. "Joshua, are you awake?"

She poked her head into the cave. "Joshua?"

The moon reflected off the sheet of cascading water and illuminated the mouth of the cave, bathing it in silvery light. Joshua's tiny cot was empty.

Allison stepped past the cot to the back of the cave. "Joshua?" The cave wall continued a few yards and stopped. Allison looked back at the tiny shelter. The blanket on the cot was neatly tucked in at the corners; the cot did not appear to have been slept in that night.

Allison ran to the mouth of the cave. "Joshua, where are you?" she screamed. But her cry was swallowed by the crash of the waterfall.

What if something had happened to him? What if he were lying somewhere, injured? The image of the bloodstained calico dress filled her mind. Allison swallowed, trying to rid herself of the bitter taste of fear that tugged at the back of her throat.

"Help me, Allison. I'm running out of time," the voice whispered in her ear. "Hurry, hurry! Find Joshua. Joshua can help."

Yes, find Joshua. That's what I have to do, she thought. *Joshua will help us.*

For more than an hour, Allison meandered through the forest, following the whispers. The farther she went, the more urgent the instructions. "Faster, Allison, faster. I'm running out of time. Hurry!"

The deeper she went into the woods, the more dense the trees and the darker the night. She could barely see branches that reached out and scraped her face. She was beginning to pant. A twig snapped somewhere behind her.

"Run, Allison, *run!*" The voice screamed in her ears. "Save me, Allison. Run!"

Panic spread through her like wildfire. Blindly, Allison tore through the forest, arms stiff in front of her, trying in vain to protect her face from the outstretched branches that ripped her skin. Her lungs burned. Her heart thundered. She began to slow.

As her bare feet slapped dead pine needles and crunched dry leaves, Allison became aware of another pair of feet, *thump-thump-thumping* behind her. Heavy, labored breathing grew closer.

"Oh, Allison, help me, please. Save me!"

The air around her seemed electrified. Drawing strength from it, Allison caught a second wind. She tucked her head and rammed through the branches. She sprinted along the forest floor. The trees appeared less dense. Moonlight filtered through the branches. On a narrow path, Allison picked up her pace. Her foot hit something. She tripped and fell forward. Her arms stretched out to break her fall.

Time seemed to slow to a crawl. She fell onto a soft mound, the wind knocked out of her, and her hands slid forward in something thick and sticky. Gasping for air, Allison pushed herself up and sat back on her heels, wiping the slimy goo on the front of the calico dress. Still in slow motion, she poked the mound before her. It was covered with cloth, and beneath the cloth was a squishy mass. Slowly she looked from one end of the mound to the other.

In the dim moonlight, empty white eyes stared up at her. A wave of nausea swept through her body, leaving her limp with fear. A scream stuck in her constricted throat. Behind her, the thumping footsteps grew closer.

"Run, Allison! Save me!"

Lightning shot through her limbs. She scrambled over the lifeless mound. Her hands and bare feet slipped on the thick slime that surrounded it. The last thing she felt as she stumbled away was the stiff, cupped hand she stepped on when she bolted from the body. As Allison veered off the path and crashed into the unmarked forest, her brain reeled with the image of the face she had seen in the moonlight: the death mask of Sadie Thompson.

Allison broke through the branches and stopped, panting heavily, at the edge of a clearing. Her throat was dry and her lungs felt as though they were on fire. Her limbs trembled. Becky's body was simply not in the athletic condition hers was in and could not take the stress. Allison's spirit alone had willed it onward.

She bent over to ease the painful stitch in her side. As she did, she noticed dark stains on the front of the calico dress. She looked down at her hands and feet. They, too, were smeared with dark stains.

Oh, God, no... it can't be happening again! Not again!

Tentatively, she lifted her hands to her face. The smell was unmistakable.

Blood.

She was covered in Sadie Thompson's blood!

Behind her, an explosion of twigs cracking and branches snapping made Allison duck beneath a clump of bushes. She peered out in time to see a figure crash through the branches and halt a few feet away.

In the moonlight stood a man, barefoot and shabbily clad in tattered shirt and pants. His back stooped, making him appear shorter than he was, arms dangling below his knees like those of an ape. He wheezed as he breathed. His head oscillated back and forth, scanning the clearing.

He turned toward Allison. She bit her lip.

The man's head was like that of a lion: A matted mane of dark hair stuck out past his ears and fell to his shoulders. A black beard that hung below his neck covered most of his face; the rest was hidden by unkempt strands of long, dark hair. The whites of his eyes, round with emotion, stared from behind the matted strands.

As the man turned away, something cold slithered over Allison's bare foot. She gasped and bit her lip harder to keep from screaming. But the man whipped around and lunged toward her. Before his arms could reach her, Allison sprang up and tore into the clearing. She could hear the man's footsteps close behind.

"Wait!" the man yelled. "Stop! Stop, I say. Come back!"

The louder the man yelled, the harder Allison ran. When she reached the other side, she plunged into the woods. All the while, another voice screamed in her ear: "Run, Allison. Save me!"

Allison stumbled through the dense cluster of branches. She tripped on roots and over logs on the forest floor. But each time she'd pick herself up and keep going. It felt as though she had been running for hours. Becky's body was ripped and scraped and bruised, but Allison ceased to feel pain.

She didn't know how long she could keep Becky's body moving. But if she was tired, the man had to be tired, too. No matter how out of condition Becky might be, the man was older and seemed to have a breathing problem. She had to keep going. Her life and Becky's depended on it.

Allison had no idea where she was headed or how far she had traveled that night. Nor had she any idea of how far she was from Magda's cottage or Joshua's cave or even the Cardona Pomales estate.

The only thing that seemed to matter now was survival.

CHAPTER 12

By the time Allison reached the edge of the forest, dawn was breaking. The terrain was rugged and dry, and she had to be careful not to trip on loose rocks. She came to a steep hillside. At the bottom of the hill, a dirt road wound along the edge of a ravine.

Although Allison had not heard her pursuer for what seemed like over an hour, she wasn't willing to take chances. Tired as she was, she crouched down and, half sitting, half squatting, slid down the loose dirt and gravel of the hillside. She had to get to the road. Perhaps it would lead her to a town or even back to the Cardona Pomales estate.

Finally, Allison reached the bottom of the hill. Trembling from terror and exhaustion, she lowered her head to her knees and hugged her legs. Maybe she could take a few minutes to rest. She glanced around. She was sitting at the edge of the dirt road, exposed on all sides. This was no place to rest. About to stand, she was startled by the sound of falling rocks.

At the top of the hill squatted the black-bearded man. He

was trying to make his way down the hill. Allison scrambled onto the road and stumbled along it, trying to get away.

"Girl! Stop, wait," he yelled. "Don't run away!"

As Allison turned to see how close he was, she stepped on a stone in the road, twisting her ankle. Hot flares shot up her leg. She stumbled. The man was gaining on her. No time! Even if she tried to hop-limp, she could never outrun him. Allison searched around for a weapon—a stick, a rock—something to protect herself.

Suddenly, a scream pierced the air. "Noo-ooo!"

Joshua catapulted from the top of the hill and onto the man's back. "Allison, run!" he yelled. *"Run!"*

Allison watched in terror as man and boy struggled in a mad tangle of arms and legs. Joshua's slight build was no match for the man. She had to help.

Spying a dead branch by the edge of the ravine, she hop-limped to the branch. As she stooped to pick it up, the ground dissolved beneath her. A scream ripped from her throat as she slid down the cliff on her belly, digging fingers and toes into the loose dirt and grabbing in vain at shrubs and rocks that whipped by. She landed on a ledge about twenty feet from the road, her right leg horribly twisted beneath her. Below lay a fifty-foot drop.

A tiny sound filled her brain and grew louder. It was the sound of weeping. Between sobs, a voice whimpered, "Oh, please save me. Please don't let me die."

Allison tried to lift her arm, but the tiniest movement sent a spray of gravel shooting off the ledge. Without touching it, she knew her leg was broken. She could never climb off the ledge alone.

"Oh, God, help me," Allison prayed. "Please let this ledge hold."

"Allison!" Joshua's scream echoed, bouncing off rocky cliff walls.

Allison heard the sound of running feet, and Joshua's head appeared above her.

"Joshua!" she cried. "Don't get too close. The ground, it's—"

"Don't you worry about me. Are you hurt? Can you move?"

"My leg—I think it's broken."

"I'll come down to you."

"No! This ledge won't hold both of us."

Joshua stood up. "I'll have to get help, then. Can you manage—"

A deep rumble from the center of the earth swallowed the rest of his words. Explosions of dirt and rocks tore through the ravine. The cliff shook as if a giant hand were jarring it back and forth. The violent motion flung Joshua off the edge. He sailed past Allison like a rag doll.

As though a trapdoor had been released, the ledge on which Allison lay split from the cliff and dropped away. For an instant she hovered, suspended in midair. In that split second, she felt Becky's terror, felt the knowledge of impending death. Then she snapped free from Becky's body and floated up into the sky.

As Becky's body plummeted through the air, Allison floated high above the scene, screaming, "Becky! Joshuuu-aaaa!"

I whirl through the wind tunnel toward the sound of sobbing. The emotional pain is unbearable; it overwhelms me, paralyzes me. But without a body, I can't shed tears, I can't let go, I can't fully release my grief.

I get it now. I finally understand how Becky can reach into the future.

Becky is dead.

She fell to her death at the ravine during the 1906 earthquake. It's her ghost that speaks to me now, that orders me back to the past to try to make things right. Her spirit can't rest with the knowledge of what she did: She led the boy she loved to his death. She has waited all these years for someone to help her undo the past.

And she chose me.

But I failed. I failed her . . . and I failed Joshua.

Floating above the hospital room, I see Mom sitting beside my bed, holding my hand. PoPo is lying in the crook of my other arm. Mom has her head on my chest, and she's sobbing. I try to float down into my body, but a force like that of repelling magnets keeps me away.

Mom, don't cry. I'm back. Please don't cry.

Mom raises her head and glances sleepily around the room. Her cheek is red from where it was pressed against my chest, but her face isn't tearstained. The sobbing continues.

Becky, is that you?

"Allison," Becky whimpers, "you were too late. I needed you to help me, but you were too late."

I'm sorry, Becky. I tried. But I didn't know what to do . . .

"I helped you, Allison. You have to help me."

There's nothing I can do, Becky. You're . . .

"You have to help me. It's your turn—"

Stop saying that! I yell, finally losing patience. *I know you helped me. I know I wouldn't be in the hospital if it weren't for you—lot of good it's done me so far. But I need to know how to help you. Just tell me how. I'd give anything to undo what happened to you...and Joshua.*

"Joshua...oh, Joshua." Becky begins to sob again, a sorrowful, haunting sob.

Then the sobbing fades, and the force field is lifted. I'm sucked back into my body with a snap. I feel Mom's hand on mine and the softness of PoPo against my other arm.

The door opens. "Mrs. Blair?" a woman's voice says.

Mom releases my hand and rises from her chair, scraping the legs on the linoleum. "Doctor, thank you for coming. Any news?"

"Mrs. Blair, Allison is going to need surgery—"

"Surgery?" Mom's voice quavers. "What kind of surgery? Is it dangerous?"

"Brain surgery. When Allison was admitted, the CT scan showed a very small subdural hematoma secondary to the accident—"

"A what? You might as well be speaking Greek. I—I don't understand."

"A small bleeder inside her head—actually, between the inside of her skull and her brain. At the time, it wasn't significant enough to require immediate surgery, especially in Allison's weakened condition."

The doctor pauses a moment, then continues. "As I've explained before, we've attributed her coma to a diffuse brain swelling that occurred because of a contusion—a bruising of her brain caused by the injury to her head when she hit the rocks. Allison was beginning to improve as her brain 'healed,' but there's been an abrupt deterioration—"

"Deterioration?" Mom whispers. I feel her sink onto the edge of my bed. "You mean, Allison's getting worse?"

"I'm afraid so, Mrs. Blair. When we repeated the CT, we found that the subdural has grown and requires an operation to drain the mass of blood. Right now, the collection of blood inside Allison's skull is putting too much pressure on her brain, making her symptoms worse."

"If you operate, could she . . . ?"

"With brain surgery, Mrs. Blair, there's always a risk. But we have no choice. Without the surgery, her brain will be irreversibly damaged, and she will likely die."

Mom and the doctor keep talking, but I've stopped listening. *I might die. Even if I don't, I might never awake from this coma. Oh, will this nightmare ever end?*

Mom squeezes my hand. "Please come back, Allison. I need you."

"I need you, Allison," whispers another voice. "I helped you, now you help me."

No! Not now! Let me be with Mom. I can't go back there—there's nothing to go back to—Joshua's gone!

Mom is still beside me, holding my hand, but her voice is muffled.

"It's time, Allison," Becky whispers.

I fight to feel Mom's hand, to hear her voice, but all I can hear is a rush of air, like the sound of a giant fan spinning, and Becky's voice.

"You have to help me, Allison. I helped you. Now it's your turn."

I feel myself lift from the bed. I struggle to reenter my body, but the force field is back. Becky's spirit has taken over.

I can't help you. I can't change the past. You're dead, Becky. I can't bring you back!

A scream rips through my soul, shaking the very core of my being.

"Noooooo! Save me!" Becky cries, as I'm hurled through the wind tunnel and plunged backward in time.

PART THREE

The Secret

I cannot rest; life's lost its thrill.
I need you back—I'll fight, I'll kill!
I'll battle death; I'll travel time,
for mere existence is a crime.
Dear God, please, take me, too!

CHAPTER 13

Allison felt the moist, fresh grass beneath her bare toes and against her legs; she inhaled the scent of pines and the smell of earth, still wet from a light spring rain. The sun gently warmed her hair and penetrated the back of the thin cotton dress.

"I'm back," she whispered to herself as she walked through the pine-encircled meadow toward the Thompson cabin.

"Becky! Becky, wait up!" called a familiar voice.

Allison turned and saw Joshua emerging from under the pines. He ran through the tall meadow grass, jumping over fallen trees and branches. He was wearing the same baggy pants and plaid flannel shirt he had worn when she first met him.

"Becky, you're late." His gray eyes twinkled with mischief.

Allison stared incredulously at the boy. "You're all right."

"Course I'm all right. Why wouldn't I be? Stop playing, Becky." Joshua gave her an impish grin, his eyes laughing all the while. He tugged at one of her braids, drawing her toward him. "Come on back before your mama sees."

Allison lifted a hand to touch his face, to make sure he was really there, but he grabbed her arm and pulled her toward the thicket of pines. She was too stunned from seeing him alive and unharmed to resist.

She let Joshua lead her away from the meadow to the pines. As they were entering the thicket, a woman's loud voice shattered the peaceful silence. "Rebecca Lee! Come on home, now. Rebecca!"

"Oh, Becky—I told you we wouldn't have time." Joshua hung his head.

It's all happening again, she thought. *Exactly as before.*

Allison grabbed his shoulders. "What day is this?"

"What does it matter—"

"Just answer my question, Joshua. What's the date?"

Joshua shrugged. "Fine. It's April 1, 1906."

Allison gave him a wry grin and shook her head. "April Fools' Day." *How appropriate. This whole thing is a practical joke fate is playing on me.*

"Stop wasting time, Becky." Joshua turned Allison toward the cabin. "You'd best git, or she'll find out about us."

Allison's mind raced. She was getting a second chance to change the past. This time she knew what would happen if she failed. "No, Joshua, I'm not—"

"Don't argue, Becky. Remember what happened last time?"

"Rebecca!" Sadie's voice grew closer.

"I'd better scat, Becky." Joshua turned. "Same time, same place, next week—don't be late!"

"No, Joshua. This time, I'm going with you."

Joshua stopped and stared in disbelief. "What?"

Allison grabbed his arm and pulled him into the woods. "Hurry, she'll be here any second."

"What's gotten into you, girl?" Joshua said, panting, after they were safely away from Sadie Thompson. "I've never seen you acting like this. Running away from your ma..."

"Listen to me, Joshua." Allison turned him toward her and took his face in her hands. "Look into my eyes."

Joshua's clear gray eyes searched hers. His dimples deepened as the impish grin grew.

"Who am I?" Allison held her breath for the answer.

Joshua's eyes opened wide. "Who are you? What kind of craziness is that? You're Becky Lee Thompson, same as always."

Allison heaved a sigh of bitter disappointment. *He doesn't remember me. The fishing hole, playing in the stream, holding hands in the woods—it's never happened. I'll have to start over, trying to get him to trust me, to believe me. And he may never feel the same. But if I'm to save his life and Becky's, I'm going to have to make him believe me!*

"Joshua, try again, please...don't you see something else...something different?"

"I see you actin' crazy."

"Have I ever acted like this before?"

Joshua's brow wrinkled. "Well, no...can't say's you

have. For the past hour you've been pulling and pushing and hiding and running. And asking crazy questions."

"And do I *look* different?"

"I guess"—Joshua's grin deepened—"your eyes are kinda fiery..."

"Yes! Fiery, that's a start—fiery."

"Becky—"

At that moment, a gray-and-black ball of fur bolted from under a bush and landed at their feet. Sitting in begging position, the little raccoon covered his masked eyes with tiny black claws.

"Bubba!" Allison squealed with delight. She stooped down and scratched Bubba's head.

"You know Bubba?" Joshua squatted next to Allison.

"Sure, you introduced us when—I mean..." Allison glanced around. "We must be close to Magda's."

"Of course, we're close to Magda's—you know that." Joshua paused, his eyebrows furrowed. "You having another spell, Becky?"

"Enough about the spells, Joshua." Allison stood up. "I'm sick of hearing about those stupid spells."

"Sorry, I just meant— You're acting awfully peculiar. When did you start liking animals?"

"Joshua, I have a lot to tell you. But first, take me to Magda's. She can help me explain."

Allison was surprised at how comforting it felt to be back at Magda's, surrounded by the smells of dried herbs and flowers and candle wax. While Bubba napped in his corner, Magda served her guests a hearty fish soup with coarse brown bread and goat's cheese.

When they had finished eating, Allison turned to

Magda. "I had Joshua bring me here today because I need your help."

Magda's serene expression remained unchanged. "How may I help you, Becky?"

Now that the moment had arrived, Allison didn't know where to start. Last time, the truth almost came out by itself, through a natural chain of events. This time, she'd have to force the truth on them, unless she could get Magda to use her powers. But how? The bruised-arm incident hadn't happened yet. And if she had her way, it wouldn't happen at all.

"I ran away from Sadie—I mean Mama."

"Ah," Magda said. She continued to watch Allison with an interested but untroubled gaze.

Joshua, on the other hand, was leaning forward on his elbows. His gray eyes were narrowed and serious.

"There's so much I have to tell you both... so much I need you to believe. I don't know how..." Allison looked down at her hands.

Magda leaned forward. "Has the danger begun, Becky?"

Allison's head snapped up. "Yes! The danger is coming—it's soon. I don't have much time."

"Whoa," said Joshua, "what danger? What are you two talking about?"

"*Ten calma,* Joshua," Magda replied softly. "Let Becky speak."

"How can I stay calm when Becky's in danger?"

"Magda," said Allison, ignoring Joshua's outburst, "take my hands. Maybe you can see something."

Magda scooted her chair closer to Allison. She took the girl's hands in hers and closed her eyes. Soon she was swaying and moaning. Joshua knelt beside them, glancing back and forth from Allison to Magda.

Magda stopped swaying and began to straighten her body. Slowly, she opened her eyes and gazed not so much at Allison as through her, as though she weren't there. Her beautiful eyes seemed hollow, blind. Allison felt an iciness growing in the pit of her stomach. Magda's gaze traveled up, above Allison's head, then around her, following the outline of Becky's body.

"What do you see, Magda?" whispered Joshua.

Magda's gaze kept traveling around Becky's body. "Your spirit has an aura of danger... of tragedy... of sorrow and regret. This body has felt a past different from yours, but its future is also filled with danger and tragedy. This is not your body. You are *la otra*—the other."

Allison exhaled, relieved Magda had once more been able to see the truth.

Joshua sank back on his heels, his face pale. "What are you saying?"

"I'm sorry, Joshua," Allison began, "I'm not Becky Lee Thompson. My name is Allison Anne Blair. I'm fourteen years old, just as Becky was—is—but I was born in 1982, not 1892."

Joshua looked from Allison to Magda, then back to Allison. "Is this some ugly April Fools' joke? Because if it is, it's not—"

"I'd never joke about something like this. And have you ever known Magda to be so cruel?"

Joshua glanced at Magda and shook his head. He had that look again of having eaten spoiled meat.

"I don't understand... What you are saying is so..." He looked back at Allison; his eyes implored her. "You *look* just like Becky—same braids, same hands, same calico dress..."

Allison nodded. "This is Becky's body—"

"What?" Joshua cried, jumping away from her as though she were a monster.

"Please, please don't look at me like that."

"How do you expect me to look at you? You're telling me you're some spirit thing from the future, and you've possessed my Becky's body?"

Allison hung her head. This was going badly, very badly. It was painful enough to go through this once, but at least the last time, they'd had a chance to bond before she told him the truth. Now all he felt for her was disgust.

"If you're not Becky, where is she?" he yelled.

Allison steadied herself. "She's in the future, in 1996, in a hospital, keeping my body alive while I'm here."

"Why? How?" Joshua turned to Magda. "Does Becky have your powers?"

"I do not think so," she answered quietly.

Joshua grabbed Allison's shoulders and shook her. "Then it's your fault! What have you done to my Becky, you—you, fiend!"

"No, Joshua, please," Allison cried. "Try to understand—"

"All I understand is that you're some kind of demon that's taken possession of my poor, innocent Becky. What did she ever do to you? Why would you want to hurt her? She'd never harm a fly."

Allison pulled away, sobbing. "I didn't do this. It isn't my fault!"

Joshua grabbed her again. "If you've hurt Becky, I'll—I'll—"

"Shhhhh, Joshua, *cálmate, mijo.*" Magda eased Joshua away and offered him a chair. "*Siéntate* and listen to the girl. Let her explain."

Joshua obeyed and plunked himself onto the chair, glaring at Allison in stony silence.

"Here—Allison, is it? Sit here and calm down." Magda handed her a lace handkerchief.

Allison blew her nose. "It was her—she sent me here."

"Becky went to the future and sent you back here in her place?" Joshua's tone was cold and sarcastic.

Allison nodded.

"How? It just don't make sense. Except for her spells, Becky's always seemed normal. How could she travel ninety years into the future?"

"She's dead," Allison whispered so softly Joshua had to lean forward.

"What?"

"Becky's dead."

Joshua stared at Allison, shaking his head. "No. She can't be. She's right here. I'm looking right at her." Joshua reached out and took her hand. "See, flesh and blood and warm. You're just having a spell, Becky, that's all. And I scared you by yelling and grabbing at you." Joshua knelt at Allison's feet. "I didn't mean to yell, Becky. I'm sorry. You gave me a fright, is all. Please come back, Becky, please come back!"

Joshua wrapped his arms around Allison's waist and held her tight, his head on her lap, sobbing.

Allison lifted a trembling hand and placed it tentatively on his soft curls. Tears slid down her cheeks. "I'm so sorry, Joshua, so sorry."

Magda came over and knelt beside them, placing her

arms around both. The three remained that way for what seemed like hours. The only sounds in the cottage were of the crackling fire and Joshua's soft sobs. Finally, Magda rose and took Joshua gently by the shoulders, helping him back onto his chair.

When Joshua's eyes met Allison's, they held a mixture of sorrow and resignation. She knew he was ready to listen.

Allison told Magda and Joshua about her accident and how Becky had helped her. She explained about her coma and the trips to the past and how Becky kept insisting it was Allison's turn to help her but never told her how or why. All the while, Joshua listened as though he were in a trance, staring at the floor and saying nothing. Magda listened without expression.

"On my last trip here, I discovered why she needs my help," Allison told them.

Joshua shifted uneasily in his chair. "Why?" He asked the question as though he'd rather not hear the answer.

"To save her from..." Allison glanced at Magda. "The danger."

Joshua finally came out of his trance. "What danger? Do you know? Have you seen it?"

Allison nodded. "I lived it," she whispered. "I felt her dying."

Joshua's face scrunched up. He covered his head with his arms and let out a deep, low moan like that of an injured animal. Allison couldn't stand to see him in such pain. She flew to his side and tried to wrap her arms around him. He stiffened and moved away. Then he bolted from the cottage and disappeared into the woods.

Allison stared at the open doorway. She felt hollow, as though someone had ripped out her insides.

"He hates me," she said, sinking to the empty chair he'd left behind. It was still warm.

"Give him time, Allison," Magda said softly. "He's not thinking about you right now. He's grieving for the girl he loves."

Allison winced. *Of course he is. He doesn't even know me. The memories I have of us have never happened, and probably never will.*

"Give him time," Magda repeated.

"Time is the one thing I can't give him," Allison said, still staring at the spot where Joshua had disappeared. "If he doesn't trust me soon, he, too, will die."

CHAPTER 14

Allison followed the forest path that led to the waterfall. Once she'd told Magda the rest of the story, Magda insisted she go after Joshua. The sun was low in the sky, and the forest was full of shadows. Birds twittered sleepily in their nests, getting ready for evening. Squirrels chattered and scolded as they scrambled from tree to tree.

Soon the forest noises were drowned by the thunderous crash of the waterfall. Allison spotted Joshua sitting on the flat boulder where he had been fishing the day she hiked up the creek. It seemed like years ago since they had splashed and laughed and played together, but in this new "reality" it had never happened.

Joshua had his head on his knees, arms wrapped around his legs. As she watched him silently, trying to decide how to approach him, he lifted his head. He gave her a questioning look, eyes full of hope.

"Becky?" he called.

She shook her head sadly. "Allison."

His shoulders slumped. "Go away," he said, putting his head back down.

Allison stepped to the squishy edge of the pool. "Joshua, please listen to me."

Joshua stood. "Leave me alone." He turned and jumped off the boulder.

Allison took another step forward. "Joshua, wait— Oh-hhhh!" Her bare foot slipped on the soft bank, sending her flopping into the water, arms and legs slapping wildly.

The long skirt of the calico dress twisted around her legs, making it hard to tread water, and the pool was too deep to feel the bottom. She fought to keep her head above water, sinking and bobbing and sputtering. As she sank once more, she felt a strong arm grip her around the neck and shoulders and drag her backward across the water.

Allison's first urge was to struggle. She felt foolish having to be saved from drowning in a still pool of water when she'd been a strong swimmer all her life. But the touch of Joshua's skin against hers felt so right, she didn't want him to let go. She went limp and allowed him to carry her to the other side and onto the shore.

He deposited her gently beside a small fire. "You all right, Becky?"

"Allison."

He grimaced, then his face softened. "You all right, Allison?"

"Yes, I'm fine. Can't resist a lady in distress?"

"Nope," he replied, adding wood to the fire, "never could."

As their clothes dried by the fire, Allison leaned back against the boulder. Joshua kept busy poking at the fire, adding wood, gazing into the forest or at the fishing hole—anything, it seemed, to not have to look at her or talk to her.

Allison sighed, frustrated. "I'm not trying to harm Becky, Joshua. I'm trying to help her. Please trust me. She sent me here to help her . . . and you."

Joshua turned. "Me? How are you supposed to help me?"

Allison looked down, unable to meet his eyes.

"Allison? Does something happen to me, too? Am I in danger?"

Joshua knelt beside her and lifted Allison's chin. Her eyes brimmed with tears. She turned away.

"All right," he said, sitting beside her. "Tell me the whole story. I'm ready now."

"Unfortunately, I'm not sure I am."

Joshua turned her to look at him. "I know I haven't made it easy for you, but you have to understand how I feel. This is the craziest thing I ever heard of. It's—it's unbelievable."

"Don't you think I know that? One minute I'm a normal fourteen-year-old riding her bike up a mountain road. Next thing I know, my mother's crying her heart out beside me, and I can't move my hand to touch her, or turn my head to see her, or even open my eyes . . ."

Allison sniffed, wiping her tears and her nose with the back of her hand.

Joshua gave a resigned sigh and placed an arm around her shoulders, drawing her close. She leaned her cheek against his bare chest, breathing in the smell of pine and smoke on his skin, and closed her eyes.

"Joshua?"

"Ummmm?"

"Do you think people have the power to change their destinies?"

"I don't know—I sure hope so. My destiny is probably to be a handyman, working at the estate, or a laborer in the vineyards. But I've got dreams, big dreams."

"What dreams?" She opened her eyes. "Tell me."

"I want to be a healer; I want to help people who are hurting."

Allison sat up. "A doctor?"

Joshua grinned. "Silly, huh? A poor boy like me."

"Oh, no, it's not silly at all. You'd make a wonderful doctor. You're smart and caring. You already know how to read and write."

"How do you know so much about me?"

"The last time, when I was with you..."

"Oh." Joshua's smile faded. "Well, it's foolish talk, anyway. Reading and writing and being smart ain't gonna pay my way to college."

"It can help. You can study hard and save your money and get a scholarship. You've got to try. You've got to!"

Joshua stared at Allison, a tiny smile beginning to tickle the edges of his mouth.

"What?" she said. "Why're you looking at me like that?"

"The fire's back—in your eyes."

"Don't make fun of me, Joshua. I mean it. You can't give up on a dream!"

"You've got so much"—Joshua paused, searching for the right word—"feelings."

Allison nodded. "It's just that when I care about something...or somebody..." She shrugged self-consciously, afraid she'd said too much.

"Maybe that's it." Joshua's eyes continued to study her face. "I've never told anybody about my dreams—not even Becky. But something about you... You really are a different person. The way you talk, the way you hold your head, the sparkle in your eyes. You're a fighter." He sighed, and his face clouded over. "Poor Becky, she's never been a fighter."

Allison thought about that. It suddenly occurred to her that although Becky had not been a fighter during life, she made a pretty scrappy ghost.

"You're wrong, Joshua. That's what you said the last time, and I believed you. Now I know different. Becky *is* a fighter. She just never lived long enough to realize her own strength. But her spirit won't die. She's waited ninety years to set things right, and I don't think she'll give up till she does."

Allison watched Joshua's face as he took in what she'd said. He stood and walked to the edge of the pool to gaze into the water. After a few minutes he said, "It's time, Allison. Tell me what happens to us."

At Magda's cottage that evening, the three of them discussed Allison's options.

"The last time," Allison said to Magda, "you said I had to follow in Becky's footsteps to find out what the danger was and what Becky wanted from me. But now that I know what she wants, I think I'm free to do things my way—to try to change the past. I just don't know where to begin or how to keep away from Sadie in the meantime."

"Then perhaps," said Magda, "you should stay here with me."

"But what about Sadie? Won't she come here?"

Joshua jumped up. "She'd better not. If she hurts you again, I'll kill her!"

Magda and Allison stared at Joshua, horrified.

Realizing what he'd said, Joshua sank back in his chair. "You think I...could I have...?"

Allison shook her head. "I don't know. I looked for you in your cave that night, but you were gone. Your bed hadn't been slept in. Sometime later, I stumbled onto Sadie's body." She shuddered at the memory.

"I've known you since you were a small child, Joshua," said Magda. "You are hotheaded sometimes but never violent."

Allison agreed. "You want to help people, not hurt them. I don't believe you are capable of—"

"Murder?" said Joshua.

Allison looked away, nodding.

"But what if it isn't murder? What if I find her hurting you again, and I try to defend you?"

"It doesn't happen that way. I didn't see Sadie that night while she was still alive. At least I didn't last time, and I don't think Becky did, either. I think Sadie didn't come home, and Becky got scared and went looking for her or for you—to talk to you or to get you to help her find Sadie. Then she stumbled on her dead body."

Joshua shrugged. "Maybe it's an accident, then. Maybe we're arguing, and I push her back and she falls and hits her head."

"Or maybe it is not you at all, Joshua," Magda said.

"There is the man—the man who chases Allison. Or maybe someone else is in the woods that night."

"Do you know the man who chases me?" Allison asked Joshua.

"Describe him again."

"He was ragged and hairy, and he looked like a savage, or an escaped convict, or a lunatic. His eyes were wild, and he wheezed."

"We get a few drifters around here, looking for work at the estate or for a handout as they pass through, but I haven't seen anybody like that."

"Remember, Joshua," said Allison, "none of this has happened yet. It's only April first, the earthquake is on April eighteenth. He still has more than two weeks to arrive, whoever he is. But whenever he does arrive, he's in the woods when I—Becky—trip over Sadie's dead body. And the thing is, wherever *you* are that night—"

"Probably walking through the woods," Joshua said. "I like to do that when I can't sleep, or when I've got something on my mind."

"Well, wherever you are, you're close enough to hear my—Becky's—screams for help because, somehow, you manage to follow her to the cliff and fight the man off. Then you try to save Becky when she"—the last moments of Becky's life filled Allison's mind, chilling her so she had to rub her arms to warm them—"falls."

Joshua winced, then shook his head. "This has to be the most peculiar thing I ever heard in my life. We're talking about things that are gonna happen in the future like they already happened."

"I know what you mean," said Allison. "Most of this

has been like a nightmare for me. But I have to prevent these things from happening if I ever expect to go back home."

"That's easy enough," said Joshua. "Now that we know what happens, why can't we just stay together that night and not go into the woods? That way neither of us gets chased or goes near the cliff."

"I don't know...," said Allison. "I can't believe it's that easy."

"I am afraid Allison's right," Magda said. "You also need to keep Sadie from being murdered. I sense she should not die this way...If she does, it could adversely affect Becky's destiny."

CHAPTER 15

The next morning, a tap at the cottage door awoke Allison. The door creaked open, and a head of chestnut curls peeked inside.

"Magda? *¿Puedo entrar?*" The lilting musical voice was unmistakable. It was Teresa Cardona Pomales.

"Tere! But of course you may enter." Magda limped toward the door.

"Why are you speaking English?" Teresa gave a delighted laugh. "Are you practicing again?"

Magda embraced her friend and motioned for her to sit. "I am always practicing. But that is not it—I have a guest." Magda pointed to Allison, who was still sitting in her makeshift bed.

"Bequita, how delightful to see you again so soon. But"—Teresa eyed the comforter and her brow puckered—"you did not go home last night?"

Allison stood and began folding the comforter. "No, I was afraid to go back, so I stayed here with Magda. Sa—Mama sounded very angry yesterday, and—"

"Ha! If she was angry last night, she will be fit to be

tied today." Tere set the basket she was carrying on the table and sat down. "What were you thinking, *niña*?"

Magda sat down. "Much has happened, Tere. Sadie seems out of control these days. When Joshua brought Becky to me last night, she was quite shaken."

"I know how Sadie treats Becky," said Tere, shaking her head. "*¡Es una poca vergüenza!* That woman should be ashamed of herself, beating a child the way she does. But I still don't understand. Sadie has acted like this many times before. Why was yesterday different?"

Allison recalled the previous afternoon, when she and Joshua had heard Sadie calling for Becky. She remembered the rage in Sadie's voice and the terror she'd felt the first time she had relived that particular incident in Becky's life.

"I decided I'd had enough. I refuse to be the scapegoat for her rage any longer. So I came back here."

Tere's eyebrows flew up, and her clear blue eyes opened wide. "I've never seen you like this, Bequita. You seem so . . . different somehow. Well, then!" Tere shook her pretty curls behind her. "What shall you do now?"

Allison shrugged. "I really don't know. I can't go back home. Joshua said we'd talk about it today, but I haven't seen him yet. Come to think of it, I don't know where he is."

Tere laughed. "That boy awakes each day before it is decent. I saw him heading toward the stables as I left the house. He had probably been working for hours."

Allison tried to hide her disappointment by inspecting her fingernails. Tere and Magda laughed.

"Certainly one thing hasn't changed about you, Bequita," said Tere. "Your heart still belongs to Joshua."

Allison's face grew warm. Apparently guessing the girl's discomfort, Magda said, "I am a terrible hostess. Look how I have forgotten to offer you something to drink, Tere. You must be thirsty after your long walk."

"*Gracias,* Magda, but I almost forgot." Tere opened the basket she had brought and began to empty its contents onto the table. "Here is some fresh goat's milk and cheese, and bread still warm from Lolita's oven. The three of us can have breakfast. Come, Bequita, sit here beside me."

Magda smiled. "You're always so thoughtful, Tere. What would I do without you?"

"You will never have to find out, Magda dear. You've been like a sister to me since Isa's illness, and then Mamá... Well"—Tere tossed her head, pushing her curls away from her face—"back to the question of thirst. I would love some of your hot goat's milk with cinnamon and honey. It will help take the chill from my bones. Early morning is cool and wet in the forest. But I adore the walk. It gives me time to think and to be free of responsibilities."

Magda raised an eyebrow. "Mmm, how is Don Carlos these days?"

Tere's laughter tinkled like a crystal chandelier in a passing breeze. "Oh, Papá, Papá! He's as much of an old bear as ever. Since I turned eighteen, he's been lining up rich old coots to court me. Four years of parading *viejos* in front of me. I stand them up, and Papá and I argue. But I can never stay angry at him for long. Anyway, I am not ready to marry."

"And your other responsibilities? Isa and Doña Ana?"

Tere stepped to the tiny window at the front of the

cottage. "Isa breaks my heart. She's like one of your dried roses. A mere ghost of her former beauty remains, and she's liable to crumble and disintegrate to nothing if she is not properly handled. Now she's insisting—

"Oh, Magda!" Tere turned, her eyes glistening with tears. "She escaped last week when the nurse fell asleep, and she wandered into her old room. She found a baby doll of hers and began to scream, 'My baby, my baby! My baby's alive!'

"Papá heard her and took her back to the west wing, but he couldn't pry the doll from her arms. She's insisting it is her baby—that her baby is alive. Magda, I don't know what's worse—when Isa sits for months in a stupor, staring straight ahead, not speaking or recognizing anyone, unable even to feed herself, or when she's in these mad frenzies, screaming and crying and accusing people of stealing her baby. Whenever I visit her lately, she asks me, 'Have you seen my baby, Tere, have you seen my baby?' Then she remembers the doll on her lap and begins to sing to it while she rocks it in her arms.

"I was only seven when Isa and your brother eloped, but I still remember how beautiful and happy she looked that day. And when Papá brought her back, how her agonizing screams filled the house and ripped through my heart."

"*Ay, qué pena,* Tere." Magda hugged her friend and led her back to the table. "What a terrible tragedy has befallen our families."

"And Mamá—*ay,* Magda, *pobre* Mamá! She lies in her bed, withering away, living more and more in the past, still believing her beautiful Isa is young and happy and well. I'm surprised she's lasted these past years. If it weren't for your wonderful herbs and potions, and the titrations you make to calm Isa—I do not know..."

As she sat back down, Tere's tears finally fell. She pulled a lacy linen handkerchief from her pocket and blew her nose. "Isa takes after Mamá. All they had was their beauty. No inner strength. Nothing but flowers in the wind, vulnerable to any passing storm."

Magda playfully tugged one of Tere's curls and let it bounce back. "Thankfully, you have much more than your beauty. You are the graceful willow that bends and yields in the storm, only to remain steadfast in its aftermath. You are tougher than Don Carlos and his crusty old *papá* put together."

The two friends laughed, and Magda changed the subject. "Becky, you must be hungry. Would you like some warm goat's milk with Lolita's special bread and cheese?"

"The bread and cheese sound good. I'm not craz—partial to goat's milk."

Tere turned her attention to Allison. "So, Bequita, let's talk about you. Where shall you stay?"

Allison shook her head. "Magda offered to let me stay with her as long as I like, but it's too much of an imposition. If I could only find a job, something that would help me pay for room and board somewhere..."

"Oh! A job!" Tere's slender fingers flew to her mouth. "I know exactly what you can do."

Magda cocked an eyebrow. "What do you have in mind, Tere?"

"Becky can come home with me." Tere clapped her hands and spun around the tiny room as she talked. "We have more than enough room. And I need someone I can trust to help me with Mamá and Isa. Becky can also be our live-in seamstress. What do you think, Bequita?"

"Are you sure? I wouldn't be imposing?"

"*Ay*, Bequita, if you only knew. You'd be doing me more of a favor than I would be doing you. I desperately need help—someone I can truly trust...and talk to sometimes. Please, say yes."

"But, your father...He doesn't like me very much."

"Oh, Papá! Don't worry about him. I can handle Papá. So, *¿qué dices?* What do you say?"

Allison turned to Magda. "What do you think? Would that be all right?"

Magda nodded and gave Allison a meaningful look. "It is a wonderful idea, Becky. It may be exactly what you need."

CHAPTER 16

"I have the perfect room for you, Becky," said Tere, as she led Allison through the maze of corridors that made up the family mansion. "You shall stay on the first floor, overlooking the rose garden."

Teresa opened a door and stood back. "Well, what do you think?"

Allison stepped into a sunny bedroom suite. Two sets of French doors, on either side of the four-poster bed, opened onto a private balcony. A small stone fireplace stood near the hall door, in front of which squatted two plush chairs and a low table.

Allison's jaw dropped. Her living room at home wasn't this big. "Oh, I couldn't—this is too much! I'm just a kid and a . . . servant."

"You may be but fourteen, Bequita, but you have great maturity. I know few people as trustworthy. And I would never consider you a servant. However, you shall be well compensated for your work."

"You mean in addition to room and board?"

"Of course, only a slave would be expected to work

solely for room and board. You shall be a valued employee."

Allison turned to Tere. "Thank you, Ter—I mean, Miss Teresa. I am very grateful for everything."

"I'll have none of this 'Miss Teresa.' My friends call me Tere. And we shall be very good friends, you and I." Tere stepped back into the hallway. "Come. Now you must meet Mamá. She's been bedridden for so many years, I do not believe you have ever met."

Allison followed Tere through another maze of corridors and past a wide staircase. They stopped in front of a massive double door. Tere tapped softly, and a tall, thin woman dressed in a long white starched uniform stepped out. A prim, starched nurse's cap perched on the top of her head. The nurse reminded Allison of a sloop's mast with its sails full and stiff from wind.

"Is Mamá awake?" Tere asked the nurse. "How has she been today?"

"*Sí, señorita,* she is awake. You may go in for a little while. This is one of her better days."

"*Gracias,* Nelda." Tere motioned for Allison to step forward. "I'd like you to meet Becky Lee Thompson. She will be helping us with Mamá and Isa."

"Hmmm." Nelda gave Allison a curt nod. "More to share the load, eh?" Then she took a seat on a chair near the door.

Tere led Allison inside a cool, dark room that smelled of incense, camphor, and candle wax. As her eyes adjusted to the darkness, Allison made out a large four-poster bed, heavy drapes hiding immense windows, and candles scattered here and there on tables and nightstands. In a corner stood a shrine similar to the one she'd seen in Magda's cottage, but more elaborate. Tall red glass cylinders in which candles flickered eerily held vigil before a statue of Madonna and child and a golden crucifix.

"*¿Mamacita, cómo te sientes?*" Tere moved to the side of the bed and bent over the stack of pillows.

A tiny gnarled hand, like the claw of a bird, crept from beneath the thick comforter and pushed it down, revealing a halo of silvery curls. Tere kissed the curls, took the tiny claw in her hands, and kissed it, too. Then she perched at the edge of the bed and stroked the silver curls, whispering and cooing in Spanish.

Not wishing to intrude, Allison stepped back into a corner, hidden by the shadows. She could hear the soft, weak voice of Doña Ana responding to her daughter's questions, but because they were whispering, she did not know what they were saying.

Tere turned and gestured to Allison. "Becky, come meet Mamá. Come."

Allison approached slowly, not knowing what to expect beneath the silver curls.

"*No veo nada,*" whimpered a soft voice.

"Come closer, Becky. Step into the candlelight. Mamá says she cannot see you."

Allison stepped into the light and froze. Beneath the comforter lay a frail sparrow of a woman. The moment she saw Allison, the woman lifted her head, exposing her face to the candlelight. Two small eyes peered at Allison above a delicate beak of a nose, and pale, petal-thin skin hung loose but smooth around a proud, uptilted chin. The longer the woman stared at Allison, the more her slim neck stretched, pushing her head upward and away from the pillows, as though she wanted to get a better look but could only move her neck.

Something seemed to click in her brain, and her small eyes opened wide. The tiny hands fluttered up to her mouth.

"Isa!" she cried. *"¡Ay, Isa, mija, ven aquí!"* She held out thin arms and continued to cry out about Isa, but Allison couldn't understand her frantic Spanish.

"Shhhh, Mamacita, shhhh," cooed Tere, stroking her mother's shoulders and pushing her back down in the bed. The more Tere pushed, the more animated the woman became, trying to peer over her daughter's shoulder to get a better look at Allison. They argued softly in Spanish, Tere apparently trying to convince her the girl she saw was not Isa, and Doña Ana becoming more agitated by the moment.

"Bien, bien, Mamá. *Shhhh."* Tere gave an exhausted sigh and turned to Allison. "Mamá is confused. She thinks you are my sister, Isa, and she wants to hold you. Would you mind playing along?"

Allison hesitated. "Uh, no, sure— What do you want me to do?"

"She wants to hug you. I'm afraid she misses Isa, and with your golden hair...in the candlelight, well..."

Tere stepped aside, directing Allison to sit on the bed. The old woman held out her arms, her faded eyes shimmering. Allison leaned forward and let the woman hug her. She gently placed her arms around the frail body, which through the fine cotton nightgown felt as warm and bony as a featherless baby bird. Doña Ana's thin arms were surprisingly strong. She clung to Allison as if she believed the moment she let go, her beloved Isa would be gone forever.

Allison's face was pressed into feathery curls that smelled of lavender. *Is this what it would be like to have a grandmother?* she wondered. Both of Allison's grandmothers had died when Allison was very young.

At long last, Doña Ana released Allison. Her eyes studied Allison's face, and she smiled. Then she took one of Allison's braids in her gnarled fingers. "*¿Trenzas?*" She looked at Tere and whispered something else Allison could not hear.

Tere sighed. "Isa never wore braids. Mamá wonders why you are wearing braids today. She would like to see your hair loose. She wants to brush it."

Allison smiled at the woman and nodded. If brushing her hair loose would make the old lady happy, she didn't mind. She wasn't crazy about wearing braids, anyway. Allison hadn't worn her hair in braids since she was eight. She removed the ragged ribbons that held the braids and unraveled her hair.

Tere handed her mother a silver hairbrush and boosted her to a sitting position, fluffing the pillows to support her back. Doña Ana chuckled like a child as she brushed the honey-gold hair. Although Becky's hair was naturally straight, wearing it constantly in braids had given it long flowing waves, thick and full.

When Doña Ana was finished brushing, she mumbled something. Allison looked questioningly at Tere.

"She wants you to stand up," said Tere, "in the candlelight, where she can admire your hair."

Allison did as she was told. She shook the luxurious hair about her shoulders, enjoying the feel of it, and glanced at Tere. The young woman was staring at her as if she'd seen a ghost. At that very moment, the door swung open. Startled, Allison turned.

Framed by the doorway, the light from the hall glowing around him, stood Don Carlos. At the sight of Allison, his expression changed from concern to disbelief, then to anger.

He scowled at Tere. "What is this girl doing in your mother's room?"

Tere rushed to her father's side. "Shh, Papá! Mamá is feeling better than she has in weeks. And we owe it all to Becky. Please, do not ruin it for her."

Don Carlos glared over his daughter's head at Allison, but when his gaze moved from her to his wife, his face softened. "We shall discuss this later, Tere. For now, take the girl and allow me to visit with your mother in private."

Without another word, the man strode in his imperious way to the side of the bed opposite Allison. Doña Ana's tiny hand disappeared in his large ones. Taking the hint, Allison followed Tere out the door.

As the door closed behind them, Allison heard Doña Ana say, *"Carlitos, mi amor, ¿viste a Isabelita?"*

Rather than take Allison back to her room, Tere led her through a different part of the house.

"This is the gallery, Becky," Tere said as they entered a wide hallway lined with paintings and tapestries on one wall and tall windows on the other. A glassed double door led to the garden beyond. "My grandfather brought all the family portraits from Spain when he built this house. Most are kept here. Some are in the library."

Allison gazed around in awe. There appeared to be

hundreds of paintings. Some life-size, others miniatures, and many more in between. The portrait of a young woman with a dog caught her attention, and she stopped to admire it.

The young woman was perched on a low stool, the full skirt of her turquoise gown surrounding her like a quiet lagoon. Golden-red curls tumbled about her shoulders, cascading from beneath a black lace mantilla that draped lightly over a high comb and hung behind her, reaching far below her waist. Her chin tilted up in the characteristic haughty manner of the Cardona Pomales family, and one of her hands poised delicately on the great head of the huge white sheepdog resting at her feet.

"That is my older sister, Isabel, and old Paco when he was still a pup. It was painted when Isa was seventeen—fifteen years ago."

"Oh," Allison replied, remembering the woman's sad story. "She's beautiful."

"That she is." Tere led Allison past the gallery and through another corridor, pointing out important rooms as they passed. Finally, they reached the kitchen.

A short, round woman bustled about, giving frenzied instructions in Spanish to two young maids.

"Lolita," said Tere, leading Allison through the kitchen, "do not be so hard on the girls. They are doing fine. Becky, come here. I want you to meet Lolita."

Tere placed an arm around Allison's shoulders. "Lolita, this is Becky Lee Thompson. She will be living with us, helping me with Isa and Mamá. I'd like you to make her some lunch. And give me Joshua's lunch. While Becky eats, I'll take it to him. I need to talk to him, anyway."

At the mention of Joshua's name, Allison perked up. "Joshua's still here?"

Tere smiled. "Yes, he's in the stable working on one thing or another. He is quite handy."

"Could I—I mean—"

"Would you like to see Joshua?"

Allison nodded, her face flushing.

"Lolita"—Tere flashed the cook a smile—"on second thought, pack us a picnic lunch for three."

Lolita glanced at Allison and cocked an eyebrow, obviously disapproving of her mistress having lunch with a stable boy and a servant girl. She turned her back on Allison and gave the two maids brisk instructions in Spanish, sending them flying about the kitchen grabbing bread and bowls and a picnic basket from the pantry.

With the basket swinging from the crook of one arm, and Allison's arm locked in the other, Tere swept through the kitchen door and into the backyard.

"I like your hair like that, Al—uh—Becky." Joshua's impish grin broadened as his gaze took in Allison's loose golden hair, rippling over her shoulders in soft waves.

Allison's ears grew warm. She shook the long tresses in front of her face, noticing what a convenient hiding place they made. She could still feel Joshua's gaze on her.

"Miz Teresa," Joshua said, the smile still in his voice, "this was real thoughtful of you."

"My pleasure, Joshua." Tere leaned against the ancient oak that provided a deep shade for their lunch. "I wanted you to know about Becky's plans. I knew you would be worried."

"It sure sounds like the right decision." Joshua turned to Allison. "What did Magda think?"

"She agreed," Allison said, tucking her bare feet under the hem of the calico dress.

"Good." Joshua stood and stretched. "Well, I'd best be getting back to work. It does my heart good to know you'll be safe, Becky."

Joshua looked into Allison's eyes, and she knew he meant he was glad that *Allison* was safe, as well as Becky.

"Joshua," said Tere, "would you mind dropping off the picnic basket on your way? I'd like to chat with Becky for a while before we go in."

"Sure, Miz Teresa. See you later, Becky. I'll look you up after dinner." Joshua grabbed the basket and trotted toward the house.

Tere pushed aside the curtain of honey-gold hair that covered Allison's face. "You have been very quiet, Bequita. Is something bothering you?"

"It's just that, well, things seem to be falling into place too easily. I guess I'm still worried about..."

"You must not worry about anything, Becky." Tere gave Allison's hand a reassuring squeeze. "We will deal with any problems when they happen, *if* they happen."

"But you've been so kind to me— I don't want to be a burden."

Tere dismissed Allison's worries with a wave of her hand. "You're a delightful companion, Bequita. And I know your helping me with Mamá and Isa will be a comfort, not a burden. Now"—Tere sat up and turned Allison toward her—"let's talk about something important—like your clothes."

Allison looked down at Becky's threadbare calico dress. "I guess I can't live here dressed like this."

"No, you cannot. So, as soon as possible, you shall sew a few summer dresses. In the meantime, you may wear some of the clothes Isa and I have outgrown."

"That's very kind." Luckily, Allison had taken sewing in eighth grade and was a pretty good seamstress. But she could only sew from a pattern. Did they have patterns in 1906?

Allison's thoughts were interrupted by a commotion near the main house.

"What's that?" She turned toward the sound.

"I do not know—"

A shrill screech attacked the young women like a swarm of bees, and the formidable shape of Sadie Thompson burst into view. "I'm going to find that good-for-nothing girl and drag her back by the hair if I have to!"

Joshua, Lolita, and the two maids ran after the angry woman.

"I'm warning you, Miz Thompson," Joshua yelled, grabbing her arm and yanking her around. "If you so much as touch Becky Lee, it'll be the last thing you do!"

"Git away from me, you worthless boy!" Sadie ripped her arm free. "This is all your doing, and don't think I don't know it. Becky Lee is a lazy girl, so she'd never do something like this on her own."

Sadie turned back to where Allison and Tere were sitting, but Joshua jumped in her path. "She should've run away years ago, way you treat her."

"I told you to git out of my way!" The huge woman flung her hand sideways, striking Joshua's face as if she were swatting a gnat. The boy went sprawling to the ground from the unexpected blow.

Lolita and the maids screamed.

"*Ay, ay, ay,*" Lolita cried.

"*¡No, señora, no!*" cried one of the maids.

Allison, who had witnessed the scene in a paralysis of fear, felt electric with rage. She sprinted to Joshua's side and knelt beside him, Tere close at her heels.

"Leave him alone!" Allison screamed, wrapping her arms around Joshua's shoulders. "Is hurting people the only thing you know?"

Sadie gave a bitter laugh. "I knew you'd come crawling out sooner or later. Did you really expect me not to come looking for you?" With lightning speed, Sadie yanked Allison up by her hair. "Now you're coming back with me. And don't ever try anything like this again."

Sadie began to drag Allison along the side of the house. With the long hair loose around her face, Allison couldn't see what was happening. She stumbled and fell to her knees, but the searing pain in her scalp continued as the woman's grip remained fast.

Behind her, Lolita and the maids screamed in Spanish, and Tere and Joshua called out for Sadie to let Allison go. Allison heard their footsteps as they ran to her side.

"Sadie, let the girl go!" Tere took a firm hold of Sadie's arm with one hand and of Allison's hair with the other. "Release her this moment, or I shall have you thrown off this estate."

Sadie let go as though she were a naughty child dropping a forbidden object. "I have a right to raise my girl as I see fit."

Joshua gently lifted Allison to her feet, holding her close.

"You have no right to abuse her," said Tere. "Becky has decided to come work for me and live here at the house."

Sadie gawked. "She can't...you can't...will she git paid?"

"Of course!" Tere's eyes flashed. "Becky shall be well compensated, and she will be a valued member of the household."

"But what about me? My eyesight ain't so good no more. Who'll help me with the sewing? I've got to earn a living, too."

"You should have thought about that before treating her so shamefully. Now leave the premises this instant."

Sadie's mouth twisted into an ugly grimace. "You fancy Spaniards with your hoity-toity ways, thinkin' you're all better'n anybody else. Just like that crazy sister of yourn, always lordin' it over me and treatin' me like dirt. My stitches ain't fine enough, the buttons are crooked, do it over, do it over... Well, I'll leave now, but don't think I won't be back—and I'll bring the law with me. Becky is still a child."

"That would be perfect, Sadie," Tere replied. "It will save me the trouble of sending for the sheriff, myself. He may not be able to stop you from taking Becky back with you, but he will be quite interested in certain items of property that have mysteriously disappeared from the house at times when you've brought by your sewing."

Sadie's face paled. "You cain't prove—"

Tere's chin shot up. "Try me."

Sadie Thompson's gaze drifted from Tere to Lolita and

the maids, then to Joshua, and finally to Allison, her scowl intensifying. "I'll get you for this—all of you." Then she turned and stomped toward the front of the house.

"Sadie," Tere called before she slipped from view. The woman turned. "I will thank you never again to set foot on this property without an invitation."

Before she disappeared around the corner, Sadie shot a glance at Allison. The look of sheer hatred hit Allison in the stomach like a fist.

CHAPTER 17

When Allison returned to her room, she found two heavy cotton dresses—one emerald-green and the other ruby-red—lying on the bed. A pair of barely worn black button-up shoes awaited her on the rug. The dresses were of the style of the time, long sleeves and long skirt *(Heaven forbid any skin should show!)*, and they were obviously of good quality.

Under the dresses, she found a cotton slip, a camisole, a corset, and two pairs of long stockings. Making a face, she hid the corset under the bed, then she pulled on a pair of stockings and tried on the shoes. They felt a bit tight. Allison buttoned the shoes with an instrument she recognized as a buttonhook. She'd seen one at a museum.

Then she slipped into the emerald-green dress. She felt for the zipper in the back and groaned. Buttons! Dozens of tiny little buttons. What a pain!

When she finished, she spun around, feeling as though she were dressed for a costume ball. Eager to see herself, she ran to the standing mirror. She gasped. Her knees turned to rubber. She had to grasp the mirror stand to keep from collapsing.

The reality of her predicament shook her with the force of an earthquake. The girl who gazed back at her from the mirror was not the perky brunette she expected to see, but a pale, thin girl with blond waves cascading down her shoulders. Her large eyes were misty green, and there was something hauntingly familiar about her face.

"Bequita," exclaimed Tere when she returned, "how lovely you look. The green of the dress brings out your eyes."

Allison fought off a little shudder at the memory of the misty green eyes that had gazed back at her in place of her own. "It was very kind of you to loan me these clothes."

Tere waved away Allison's words with the flick of her hand. "Nonsense. I'm glad you can make good use of them. Come," she said, leading Allison along a wide hallway. "Now you must meet my sister, Isa."

They stopped at a wrought-iron gate. "This is the west wing. Papá keeps it locked so Isa will not go wandering."

At the look of surprise on Allison's face, she added, "For her own protection. I know it sounds cruel, but... well, wait until you get to know her before you judge us too harshly."

"Oh, please—I didn't mean to question your judgment. It's just that—well, you seem so fond of your sister."

Tere unlocked the gate and led Allison inside, relocking the gate behind her. The metallic *clang* of the closing door reverberated through the long hallway.

"I love my sister dearly. And I miss who she was and what she might have been. I've needed a young woman around all these years—someone with whom I could share my hopes and dreams. That is why I visit Magda so often. But Isa..." Tere's voice trailed off as she shook her head sadly.

"Is she dangerous?"

"Only to herself," Tere replied cryptically. Then seeming to realize Allison's true meaning, she said, "Do not worry, Becky, Isa is not to be feared, only pitied."

When they turned the corner, Allison thought she heard a soft hum. As they drew nearer, she realized it was the sound of someone humming a sad melody. At the end of the corridor, a different nurse, equally as stiff and starched as Doña Ana's nurse, sat on a wooden chair, crocheting what appeared to be fine white lace along the edges of a delicate linen doily.

"Socorro," said Tere, marching up to the nurse, "how is my sister, today?"

The nurse dropped her crocheted doily onto the table beside her and stood. "*Un poquito mejor, señorita.*" Then glancing at Becky, she translated. "A little better."

"*Bien,*" Tere said with a satisfied nod. "Socorro, this is Becky Lee Thompson. She will be helping us care for Isa and Mamá. It will be a great comfort to me to know that Becky is here to help you when I go away next week."

"Next week?" said Allison, alarmed by the news. "I will be here alone?"

Tere took Allison's arm and led her away from the nurse. "Do not worry so, Becky. You will be fine. I need to do my spring shopping in San Francisco."

Allison's heart jumped to her throat. "San Francisco?" she squeaked.

Tere's brow furrowed. "Why are you so upset, Becky? I will only be gone one week."

"Will you be back before the eighteenth?"

"Why, I believe so. Unless I'm detained—"

"No! Please, please come back before the eighteenth."

Tere glanced at Socorro, who quickly looked away. "We shall talk about this later, Becky. Come, I need you to meet Isa now."

Tere led Allison across the hall and opened the heavy door. The sound of clear, soft singing drifted out. Inside a suite similar to Tere's, a slender woman spun around, dancing with an imaginary partner.

Isa's long silk gown swept the floor in time to the ballad she sang. Golden-red curls spilled down her back in a furious tumble and leaped from the sides of her head like tongues of flame.

In the midst of a spin, Isa threw back her head and laughed—it was a high-pitched sound with a nervous undertone that grated Allison's nerves as if she'd run fingernails across a chalkboard. "José, José, *cuánto te amo*." She giggled and spun in a tighter and tighter circle, her hair flying wildly. "I will never love another, Joselito. Never let me go. Spin me, spin me, spin me!"

Isa collapsed on the floor, laughing her nerve-grating laugh.

"*Ay*, Isa, Isa!" Tere ran to her sister and sat her up. "You must be careful. You could hurt yourself."

"I was dancing with José, Tere. José would never let me be harmed. We were having such a delightful time. Let me see him again. José? José, where are you?" Isa's hazel eyes opened wide; her gaze darted erratically about the room. "José! Come back, José!"

"Shhhh, Isa," whispered Tere. "José had to go. You need to rest, so he left you to rest."

"But he will be back?" Isa peered over Tere's shoulder, searching the room. "He must come back. I need him."

"Come, Isa, let me put you in bed. Becky, help me lift her."

Together, they half carried, half dragged the struggling woman to the bed. It was then that Allison noticed the bed was stripped of linens.

Allison glanced around the room. It was bare of everything but heavy furniture. No vases. No statuettes of the Virgin or of saints. No candles or rugs or pillows. Even the drapes were missing from the French doors. The large suite held only a four-poster bed, one nightstand, a hard sofa, and two heavy wooden chairs.

"Tere, Tere, tell me, promise me José will be back." Isa's voice quivered, and her hands flew near her face like frightened birds.

"José wants you to rest now, Isa. That is all you should think about. You want to make him happy, don't you?"

Isa nodded nervously and giggled. "He loves me. José wants to take care of me. He will be back soon, won't he, Tere? Then he will take me to Spain, and we shall send for Magda. And you, Tere. Would you like to come with us? We will be far, far away from here. Far from this detestable estate and far from Papá."

"*Duérmete,* Isa." Tere pushed Isa back onto the bare mattress. "Lie back and sleep. Shhhh, sleep."

Tere stroked her sister's brow, and Isa closed her eyes.

"You are a good sister, Tere. Such a good—" Isa's eyes snapped open. She sat up. "Papá! You must not say anything to Papá. He will spoil everything. Why does Papá hate José so? José is kind and smart and brave. And he loves me. Papá should be proud to have him as a son-in-law."

"Shhhh, Isa." Tere tried to pull her sister back down, but Isa resisted. "How would you like some of Magda's medicine? It will help you sleep."

"No, I cannot sleep. I must stay awake. José is coming to take me away. I must remain alert or Papá will spoil—"

"Isa, listen to me. José will not come tonight. He wants you to rest, remember?"

"Rest?" Isa nodded, lying back and closing her eyes. "José wants me to rest."

"Becky," Tere whispered. "Come here and sit beside her. Stroke her forehead while I get the medicine ready."

Allison obeyed. As she stroked Isa's brow and hair, she noticed the deep lines of sorrow that marred the once-perfect face. Strands of silver were beginning to show around the woman's temples, blending with the red-gold curls. Softly, Isa began to hum the haunting tune Allison had heard earlier.

"Do you hear a baby cry?" Isa whispered, her eyes still closed.

Allison jumped, startled by the unexpected words. Isa opened her eyes and looked up at Allison. Their eyes locked.

Isa lifted her hand and touched a strand of Allison's golden hair. Then she stroked Allison's cheek with a trembling finger. The tiny puckers between her eyebrows relaxed.

Isa's eyes filled with hope. "Have you seen my baby?"

"Why are there no linens in Isa's room?" Allison asked Tere as they walked back to Allison's room. "And other things are missing—personal things."

Tere gave Allison a tight smile. "You are very observant, Bequita. My sister"—Tere paused, and a look of deep sadness crossed her face—"Isa poses a constant threat to herself. You saw how she was when we entered her room. Wild and uncontrollable. And this was one of her better days. She cannot be trusted alone."

"I don't understand. How would linens and a few trinkets around the room harm her?"

"*Ay*, Bequita, you are so innocent. Perhaps I should not expose you to such misery at your age. But it seemed you needed my help as much as I need yours."

In response to Tere's words, the hair on Allison's neck and arms rose as if a cold wind had passed through her. Becky's words filled her brain: *I helped you, now you help me.*

"Would you prefer not to help with Isa?" Tere studied Allison.

Allison recalled the tragic Isa and how kind Tere had already been to her. "No, I'd like to help with Isa. I don't mind."

Tere let out a sigh of relief. "I am glad. *Gracias*, Bequita. But there will be times—much more difficult times than today. Isa becomes despondent. She cries and begs to die. She has tried to harm herself several times. Once she broke a vase and cut her arm. Another time she pretended to be asleep and later tied the night nurse with the linens from her bed. Then"—Tere gazed down the hall—"she took the ropes from the drapes, and, if Papá had not entered at that very moment, she would be dead."

Allison shuddered at the thought. "I'm sorry. I didn't know."

"That is why we removed everything from the room except the heavy furniture. Isa is very clever. We cannot take any chances."

"But doesn't she get cold without a blanket?"

Tere again led the way down the hall. "We give her a sleeping sedative. When Isa is asleep, the night nurse covers her and remains in her room until morning. The blanket and pillow are removed before she awakes. Sometimes, when she becomes unmanageable, her wrists must be restrained."

"Restrained?"

"Tied to the bedposts." Tere shook her head. "It is so sad. Mamá used to become ill after each encounter with Isa. It broke her heart to see her beautiful daughter restrained like a savage. Papá has forbidden Mamá to see her."

"She can't see Isa at all?"

"It has been five years since Mamá has seen Isa."

They continued through the corridors in silence until they reached Allison's room.

"Now, what is this about my not going to San Francisco?" Tere said, attempting a smile.

"I just—I'm a little nervous about being here alone—without you, I mean. Your father doesn't like me, and—"

"Do not concern yourself about my father. I will speak to him. Isa and Mamá have taken well to you. That is what is important. Papá seems like a bear, but he is really a pussycat."

More like a cougar, Allison thought.

"But why did you want me back before the eighteenth?"

Allison struggled to find the right words. "I had a feeling..."

Tere cocked an eyebrow. "A premonition? Like Magda's?"

"Well, maybe not quite like Magda's, but yes, a premonition. A very, very strong one." Allison's eyes pleaded with Tere. "Please promise to be back before the eighteenth."

"What kind of premonition?" Tere's eyes narrowed as she studied Allison's face.

"You don't believe me?"

"I take premonitions very seriously, Becky. I simply need to know what you feel."

"Danger," Allison replied, recalling Magda's premonition about Becky. "Very serious danger, and maybe... death."

CHAPTER 18

It's so sad, Joshua," Allison told him as they strolled in the rose garden after dinner. "I think Isa even tried to hang herself. And all because of that ultra-controlling father of hers. He won't even let her mother visit her."

"I've heard her crying sometimes," said Joshua, "in the evening or in the early morning. It's the spookiest sound I ever heard. First the wailing, like a baby crying, then the sobbing. About rips out a feller's heart to hear it. Makes you feel so helpless."

"If I could only get through to Isa," Allison continued. "I'd like to make a difference with her while I'm here. But what can I do? In the future we've got some incredible shrinks—psychiatrists, doctors of the mind—but even they have trouble curing mental illness."

"Tell me about the future, Allison," Joshua said.

Allison perched on a cement bench. Joshua joined her. She breathed in the scent of roses and cool night air as she decided what to tell him first.

"There are wonderful things, Joshua, incredible things. By 1970, we'd gone from what was considered science fiction to reality." Allison turned to Joshua, her eyes sparkling. "Joshua, an American astronaut walked on the moon!"

Joshua's eyes opened wide. "The moon! Nah, you're just fooling—"

"No, it's true!" Allison felt as giddy as if she'd just walked on the moon herself. "And we've got satellites traveling in space, taking photographs of other planets and sending them back. We've got a thing called television—an electric box with moving pictures on a screen in the front, and microwave ovens that can bake a potato in less than ten minutes, and an electronic brain that holds information from thousands of books and looks like a small, flat typewriter, and airplanes that fly us from San Francisco to New York in half a day—"

"Whoa, whoa! My head is spinning. Sure you're not making this up?"

"Oh, no, Joshua, and there's so much more." Then Allison's smile faded. "But for all the good things, there's bad, too. So much violence: Our country becomes involved in two world wars and three other major wars. When Mom was my age, she never felt afraid to go to school. Schools were safe and clean. Now some kids carry guns to school, and drugs... Kids are dying all the time, killing each other—little kids, younger than us. Some kids live with the fear they'll never grow up. My school's pretty good, but you hear about the others."

"Why don't they just not go to school?"

"Can't. For one thing, it's the law—kids have to go to school. For another, without an education— Well, you know how bad you want to be a doctor? Can't do that without going to school."

Joshua nodded somberly. "Like Magda says, sometimes you gotta take the good with the bad. It sure is a shame. The future sounded like paradise. Tell me more of the good things."

Allison thought for a moment, then she smiled. "I know something you'll like. They've made great strides in medicine. Scientists have discovered how to prevent some diseases, like polio and smallpox, and how to treat others, like infections, pneumonia, and tuberculosis. They're always looking for cures to new, deadly diseases. And"—Allison lowered her voice to a whisper, as if she were telling a ghost story—"they can transplant organs from dead animals or humans to other humans."

"Transplant?" Joshua looked green.

"They can take a baboon's heart and sew it up in a living person, in place of his sick heart. And they can take a human heart or liver or other organ from someone who's just died, and they sew it inside a living person."

Allison watched Joshua digest the information. His mouth gaped. "I'll be tied to an anthill and left for dinner. Putting a dead person's heart in a living person!"

Allison's tone grew serious. "My dad was on the waiting list for a new heart—he had a bad heart—but he died before he got it." Allison smoothed her emerald-green skirt as she swallowed a sob.

"That's a real shame, Allison." Joshua scooted closer to her and placed an arm around her shoulders. They sat silently for a few minutes, listening to the croaking of a frog in the distance. Then he said softly, "What about you? What are the doctors doing for you?"

Allison told him about her impending brain surgery, then went on to explain about the coma. "I've heard about comas on television. Sometimes people lie in the hospital for years and never wake up. Other times, they wake up after a few days or months, or even years. I just hope I've got a really good neurosurgeon—that's a doctor who operates on the brain."

Joshua took her hand in his. "I hope so, too, Allison."

She noticed again how perfectly her hand fit in his. Then another thought occurred to her: It was Becky's hand that fit so well, not hers. *Would my hand fit as nicely?* Maybe that wasn't important. Maybe the fact that their spirits seemed to mesh was all that mattered.

"I hope your dreams come true, Joshua. I hope you become a doctor."

"Maybe"—Joshua's expression grew intense—"if I live through the earthquake, maybe I could become one of them brain doctors and study real hard, so I'd be ready to operate on you after the accident."

"What a sweet thing to suggest." Allison felt a warm glow radiate inside her chest. "I'm afraid it won't work, though. My accident is ninety years from now. That would make you—"

"A hundred and five years old," said Joshua, his shoulders drooping. Then he perked up. "Do people live that long in the future?"

Allison grinned. "No. More people live longer than they do now, until about eighty or ninety. Any older is rare. And no offense, Joshua, but I'd rather not have a really old man operating on me, no matter how good a surgeon he was when he was young."

"I suppose you're right," Joshua said with a sigh. "What are you going to do—if everything goes well? Marry some feller and settle down?"

Allison snorted, pushing him away. "No way! At least I won't marry until I have a career. Even then, I won't 'settle down'! Women don't do that in my time. But I'll tell you—even if I had to live in your time, I wouldn't just marry and have babies, and stay pregnant and barefoot in the kitchen."

At the word *pregnant*, Joshua's face reddened.

Allison laughed. "Sorry, I forgot to act like a demure young lady."

"I reckon I never heard a girl talk like you. Well, other than Miz Teresa, who's kinda hotheaded."

"Women are people, Joshua. Smart, capable people. People who count and are important to society. Men can't go around bullying us and thinking for us and telling us to keep quiet the way Don Carlos does with his wife and daughters. Be prepared for a shocker. In the 1920s, women finally gain the vote. Imagine, Joshua, the slaves were freed, and it *still* took another fifty-some years for men to allow women to be counted! Then in the 1960s, the women's liberation movement begins, and women speak out and stand up for equal rights in the workplace and in society. If you're a man—watch out!"

"After meeting you, I believe it," Joshua said with a laugh. "Do all girls in the future think like you?"

"A lot, but not all. Some women still think feminism is a dirty word."

"Feminism?"

Allison considered for a moment whether she should start a discussion on the equal rights of men and women. Even in the nineties, she'd gotten into heated arguments with her teachers and some boys in school over women's rights. She knew what Don Carlos would say about feminism, but Joshua was young, and he seemed so open-minded and eager to embrace new ideas. Why not? If she could convert one man in 1906...

"Being a feminist means that you believe that men and women should have equal rights under the law and in the workplace," Allison went on to explain.

"Whoa, whoa, whoa!" Joshua cried, staring at Allison, his eyes starting to bug out. "You believe all that? That women should be doctors and lawyers and fight in wars?"

"I don't think *anyone* should fight in wars, but if a man *has* to and a woman *wants* to, then yes. But let me finish."

Joshua was continuing to stare, his mouth gaping, but Allison ignored him and plowed ahead.

"I think the problem is that some women seem to think being a feminist means that you are some kind of man-hating, picket-sign-carrying type who marches in demonstrations and burns her bra and yells a lot about how badly she's been treated."

"Burns her what?"

Allison glanced at Joshua, who looked as if he'd just staggered off a sailboat that had been caught in a storm, and grinned. "Trust me, Joshua, you don't want to know. Anyway, if a girl has ever been told that she's not as smart as a boy or that she's not good at math or science because she's a girl or that she can't play in a game she wants to play in because it's for boys or that she can't go somewhere because she's a girl, and if she's ever thought, *That's not fair!* she's thought like a feminist.

"My mom didn't think she was a feminist until she had to start working again after Daddy died. Even though she was smarter and a better accountant than some of the men in her firm, she didn't earn as much money, and she got passed over for promotion by a guy who started working for the company five years after she started. So she quit, and she's working for herself. That's all feminism means, a belief that men and women should have the same rights."

Joshua was shaking his head. "This all makes my head spin. All the women I've known have been wives and mothers and—"

"No, Joshua. Think about it. Magda is a healer. And Tere is, well, Tere is her own person. She doesn't do what her father wants—she does what *she* wants. Maybe she'll be a wife and mother, maybe she won't. But whatever she does, it'll be *her* decision, I just know it. Even Isa rebelled because she wanted to marry the boy she loved, not someone mandated by her father. All I'm saying, and all that feminists are saying, is that women should be allowed to think for themselves the way men are allowed to make their own decisions."

Joshua nodded. "Magda's a healer... I never thought of it like that. It's so natural for her, but I just think of her like my second mother."

"That's just my point, Joshua. Women can be mothers, *and* they can have a job doing something they love."

"So what *are* your plans?" he said with a look of dread in his eyes. "Not a soldier or a sailor or a pirate, I hope."

Allison grinned. "I told you, I don't believe in war. Although a pirate on the high seas might be fun."

A look at Joshua's face made her break out in giggles. At the sound of her laughter, Joshua relaxed, and the humor returned to his eyes.

When she stopped laughing, Allison shrugged. "I'm not sure what I want to do. I haven't decided yet. The way I carry on about people's rights, Mom says I should be a civil rights lawyer. But I love nature and animals and the open air too much to sit in a stuffy old office or law library. I can find another way to fight for civil rights. I'd rather be either a forest ranger or a veterinarian—an animal doctor."

"Animal doctor," Joshua repeated, considering.

"Or a forest ranger. I'd work for a national park and help take care of the animals and the environment. I wanted to work as an intern this summer—to see how I liked it. I was going for an interview with the ranger above Devil's Drop when the car—a sports car, much faster than the motor cars you have now—hit me and sent me flying down the cliff."

Joshua winced at the reminder of how Allison's accident had occurred. He took her hand again and squeezed it tight. "We've got to get through this, Allison. You and Becky and me. Alive."

That night, before getting ready for bed, Allison stood before the mirror. She shuddered as she examined the strange face and figure. It was still a shock to look into a mirror and not see her own face gaze back. And she couldn't rid herself of the feeling she had seen that face before, somewhere other than on the girl in the mirror.

"How grand you look, Allison," Joshua had told her that evening when he first saw her in the emerald-green gown. "Just like a lady—like you belong here, in this mansion." His eyes and impish grin were more teasing than ever as his gaze traveled the length of her gown and back up to her loose golden waves, resting finally on her face.

Being inside Becky's body felt like being in her own body. It was easy to forget her true physical appearance. So when Joshua complimented her, she had blushed, blossoming under his admiring gaze. But now she was reminded that each time he complimented her, it was really Becky he was complimenting.

As Allison shed the green gown and slipped into the simple white cotton nightgown Tere had given her, she continued to ponder her predicament. It was one thing to live in another person's body without knowing what you look like—almost like playing make-believe. But looking in the mirror reminded her that this was no game: Allison Anne Blair's spirit was locked in Rebecca Lee Thompson's body until her debt to Becky was paid or until Allison, herself, was dead.

Allison opened her eyes. She was in a strange bed, in a dark room. As her gaze slid over the unfamiliar furniture, the sound of voices drifting through the open window dragged her attention from her surroundings. She padded barefoot over the cold tiles to the window.

A full moon cast its silvery glow over the rose garden and lawn. Agitated voices continued, somewhere around the corner of the building. Remembering where she was and why she was there, Allison ran to the French doors and slipped outside, rushing amid the shadows, following the sound of the voices.

"Understand me, woman!" said a man's voice. "I will *not* be blackmailed. Now get off my property this instant!"

"You won't be so hoity-toity when your precious secret is out and—"

"Listen to me"—the man spoke through clenched teeth—"if you ever breathe a word of this nonsense to anyone and upset the members of my family, it will be the last word you speak!"

"Nonsense, eh?" The woman gave a short, bitter laugh. "If it was such nonsense you wouldn't be so riled up."

"It *is* nonsense. Nothing but a nasty lie dreamed up by a scheming, greedy woman to avenge her jealous nature and profit from the misery of others."

"Lies or not, do you want your precious Tere and Isa and your dear Ana—"

"Never! You hear me—never utter the names of my family again! I will pay to get you out of our lives. But don't *ever* let me catch you on my property again as long as you live!"

The woman snorted. "You think you're so high-and-mighty. Well, you'd better pay up."

"Madam, I have given you my word, and the word of a Cardona Pomales is solemn."

"Humph! I'll contact you—"

"I shall be the one doing the contacting, and after that, I never want to see you again. Is that clear? Now get off my land!"

The woman snorted once more. Allison peeked around the corner in time to see the bulky form of Sadie Thompson turn and hobble away from the stiff and formidable figure of Don Carlos.

In the shadows opposite where she stood, Allison noticed a crouched figure, who also had been listening to the argument, rise and slip from view.

CHAPTER 19

An urgent knocking at Allison's bedroom door dragged her from a heavy sleep. "Becky, wake up! Becky!"

Pale morning light barely illuminated the room. The early morning twitter of birds floated through the open window.

The insistent knocking continued.

Allison slid from her bed and unlocked the door. She'd locked it the previous night due to a case of jittery nerves. The moment she cracked open the door, Tere burst inside.

"Isa is missing. She must have escaped during the night. Socorro and I have searched the entire house, with no sign of her. She must be in the woods."

"How could she escape?"

Tere waved a hand impatiently. "A window perhaps—that is not important right now. First, we must find her, later, we can worry about how she got away."

"It'll just take me a minute to dress," Allison said, forgetting how long her new clothes took to put on. "Is Joshua here yet? Maybe he can help."

"A very good idea. I will have Socorro and the maids

search the rest of the estate, then I will look for Joshua. We shall meet you at the front gate." Tere rushed off, leaving Allison alone with the task of getting dressed.

When she lifted the green dress and spotted the dozens of tiny buttons that had to be dealt with before she'd be ready, she tossed it aside and slipped on Becky's old clothes. Threadbare, maybe, but they were quicker and more practical in an emergency.

"Boy, could I use some good old blue jeans and a T-shirt right now," she muttered as she ran barefoot through the corridors of the mansion.

Joshua and Tere were waiting for her at the gate. At Tere's raised eyebrow, Allison explained, "There wasn't time to do all those buttons."

"I suppose you are right," Tere replied. "We must not waste time. We must find Isa before she harms herself. Joshua, you know these woods better than anyone. Where should we start?"

"Did Miz Isabel like to walk in the woods when she was young? Maybe she had a favorite spot or a secret hiding place."

Tere gasped. "Magda's cottage! Isa was upset last night because she insisted José was coming for her. Maybe she went looking for him."

"Why, sure!" said Joshua. "He used to live at the cottage with Magda. It would make sense for Miz Isabel to look there."

Joshua led them along his shortcut through the woods. When they reached the cottage, Isa was sitting in Magda's rocker, rocking and singing to a ragged-haired baby doll on her lap. Magda perched on a stool at her side.

As they entered, Isa leaped from the rocker, her eyes anxious and searching.

"José?" she said, running to the door and looking past the three visitors. "José, where are you?" She turned to Tere. "Have you seen José?"

"Come back in the house, Isa," said Tere, taking her sister by the shoulders and leading her to the rocker. "*Siéntate*. José cannot come today."

Isa shook her head like a spoiled child who is reminded of bedtime. "José is coming, I know it. I must be patient. He promised he would come for me, and José would never break a promise."

Tere turned to Magda, her face etched with concern. "What can I do?" she said, sinking onto a chair beside her friend. "I simply do not know what to tell her without breaking her heart again."

"What is there to tell her?" Magda replied. "She lives in a fantasy world, believing her beloved José will come back for her and make everything right. Perhaps it is kinder to leave her in that world. Somewhere inside, she knows the truth, and perhaps when she is ready to face it, she will."

Tere squeezed Magda's hand. "You are wise, dear Magda."

The two friends turned to watch Isa rocking her baby doll in her arms, cuddling it close while she hummed and cooed to it.

Allison took Joshua's hand and led him to the door. "Let's go outside while they visit," she whispered. "I have something to tell you."

"Last night," Allison told Joshua, "I was awakened by angry voices. I snuck out to see who it was."

"So who was it?"

"Sadie and Don Carlos! Out in the shadows of the rose garden. Can you believe it? Sadie is blackmailing him."

"Blackmail? What could she have on Don Carlos?" Joshua said, more to himself than to Allison. "Not that he's any saint. Lord knows he probably has his share of ugly secrets—that kind of man usually does. But how would Sadie find out?"

Allison shrugged. "All I heard was it's some secret that would upset his family. Don Carlos tried to pretend he didn't care what Sadie knew and that she was making it up. But I could tell by his voice that he was afraid of anyone finding out this secret. When Sadie threatened to tell his wife and daughters, he finally agreed to pay her off. Then he told her to get off his land and never come back."

Joshua snorted. "Miz Teresa told her that, too, but she sure didn't lose time in crawling back there like a snake after a rat."

Allison thought about that. "Why do you suppose Sadie is so nasty? You should have seen the look she gave me yesterday, after Tere told her never to come back." She shuddered at the memory. "It gives me the willies just to think about it. She really hates poor Becky—and she's her mother."

"Her stepmother," Joshua informed her.

"Sadie is Becky's *step*mother? What happened to her real mom? And where's her dad?"

"Both dead. Magda says Becky's ma and pa were real good folks. Kind and generous, though they was dirt poor. Her ma, Ruth, died of consumption when Becky was five. Then her pa needed a ma for Becky so he married Sadie. I hear she wasn't so bad then. Two years later, Ned Thompson died of influenza. That's when the trouble began."

"Trouble?"

"Well, Magda says Sadie was always as crusty as an old muddy boot, but after Ned died, she became bitter and mean. She resented Ned for dying and leaving her to fend for herself and care for his kin. At least he left her the cabin and a little piece of land. Becky says that soon after her pa died, the beatings began."

"How sad for Becky. Being orphaned and left with that woman."

Joshua smiled sadly. "Being orphans was one of the things that brought us together. But at least she had the memory of loving parents, and I had Magda."

"Then Becky got stuck with Sadie." Allison sighed. "I wish I could've caught more of the conversation between Sadie and Don Carlos. We don't know what the secret is or when the payoff is. Any bit of information concerning what Sadie says or does in the next two weeks could be important."

"Why should it matter what Sadie says or does?"

"Because, Joshua, if Magda's right, we have to find out who wants to kill her and prevent it from happening. That reminds me. While they were arguing, someone else was hiding in the shadows, listening to them. Just after Sadie left, the person disappeared."

"Could you tell who it was?"

She shook her head. "Couldn't even tell if it was a man or a woman."

Allison remembered something else. She gasped and grabbed Joshua's hand. "Joshua, I almost forgot. The last time I came back—the day of April seventeenth—you were going to take me to the Thompson cabin. We got to the edge of the woods, when we heard a door slam. It was Don Carlos, leaving the cabin. He rode off in a huff, and Sadie came out carrying something she apparently hid in the woods. We never found out what happened, because you insisted I go back to Magda's. That's the night Sadie was killed."

"What are you trying to say?"

"I'm not sure. I just know Sadie Thompson is quickly becoming Public Enemy Number One. It might even be Don Carlos who clips her off. He certainly sounded like he wanted to do her in last night!"

"Don Carlos is heavy-handed, all right," Joshua agreed. "But murder?"

"*Someone* kills her, Joshua. And one thing is for sure—Don Carlos hates her, and blackmail is a perfect motive for murder."

As Allison and Joshua escorted Tere and Isa through the forest and back to the estate, Allison thought about the last moments of their visit with Magda. She and Joshua had still been talking outside the cottage when they heard a heart-wrenching cry.

They had rushed inside to find Isa kneeling in front of the still-swaying rocker. On the floor in front of her lay the bedraggled baby doll, arms stretched upward in a perpetual and pathetic plea for affection. Isa's hands covered her face, and her entire body shook with sobs.

When Tere stooped to wrap her arms around her sister, Isa shoved her away. "No! Don't touch me! You are part of it. You know where my baby is, and you refuse to help me find her."

"Shhhh, Isa," said Tere, trying to scoot closer to her sister. "Here she is—in front of you. Here is your baby."

Isa slowly raised her eyes, and when she looked at Tere they were full of contempt. "That is no baby!" Her words had a hollow, accusing tone. "That is a stupid doll! My baby is alive and needs me, but I cannot find him... her?" Isa's voice softened to a whimper. When she spoke again, she spoke mostly to herself. "The nuns would not tell me whether it was a girl or a boy. I still do not know. Papá forbade anyone to tell me. Can you believe that?"

She looked back at Tere, then at Magda. " 'The baby is dead,' Papá said, 'so what does it matter?' Well, my baby is not dead! I know it! A mother would know!" Isa shrieked the words and turned to face her sister, holding out her arms.

"My arms ache to hold my baby. I heard it cry the day it was born, and I hear it cry every day of my life. Each cry is etched in my heart. My baby is out there somewhere, and nothing you say will convince me otherwise. But José will help me. José and I—together we shall find our baby."

"Isa, *por favor,* I beg you..." Tere stretched out a hand to Isa. "Believe me—"

"No! I will believe no one but José. Soon, José will come."

Tere rose and clung to Magda, her lovely face twisted with pain. "I don't know what to do, Magda. What shall I do?"

Magda helped her to a chair and turned to Isa. "Isabelita, it is Magda. Remember Magda?" She knelt beside the sobbing woman.

Isa nodded and gave her old friend a lost, trusting look. "José loves you, Magda."

Magda smiled. "And he loves you, Isa. He wanted us to trust and take care of each other, remember?"

"José wants me to trust you," Isa repeated as if in a trance.

"Come, *siéntate,* sit back in the old rocker, and let me pour you some sweet chamomile tea. Then you can tell me all about the baby, how is that?"

Like an obedient child, Isa allowed Magda to lift her onto the rocking chair. As Isa sat back, she grabbed Magda's shoulders and drew her close, clinging to her and whispering, "Help me find my baby, Magda. Help me find my baby."

When Magda finally pulled away from Isa, she had a strange look on her face. It was the same look she'd had when she had "seen" into Becky's and Allison's pasts.

Allison watched Magda carefully, waiting for an opportunity to ask her about it. She saw Magda add some drops of liquid from a tiny blue vial to Isa's tea. She also noticed how Isa's fluttering hands and shaking shoulders became calm soon after she finished her tea.

While Tere and Joshua prepared a sedated Isa to leave the cottage, Allison took Magda aside.

"You saw something when Isa held you. What was it?"

Magda glanced at Tere. "You mustn't say anything to upset Tere or Isa."

"I won't, I promise."

Magda leaned forward and whispered into Allison's ear. "I saw Isa during labor. I felt her joy when she gave birth, and I felt her sorrow when the nuns told her the baby was born dead. But Isa is right, the baby was not stillborn. I, too, heard the baby cry."

CHAPTER 20

Allison helped Tere get Isa to her room. The drops Magda had put in her tea had not only sedated the woman, they made her sleepy. After the long walk through the woods, Isa could barely stand. While Tere and Allison put Isa to bed, Socorro moved her wooden chair into the bedroom, preparing to watch over her.

Tere was visibly shaken by the experience and retired to her own bedroom to rest. Allison took advantage of the time alone to change into the ruby-red gown. Once she had dressed, she combed her hair, tied it back with a red satin ribbon, and set off to explore the mansion.

As Allison approached the library, male voices drifted toward her. She noticed that the door next to the library stood ajar and that the voices seemed to be coming from the room behind the door. Glancing around to make sure no one else was in the corridor, she tiptoed to the edge of the doorway.

"But Don Carlos," said a man whose voice Allison did

not recognize, "I do not understand. You wish to withdraw one hundred dollars in gold coins?"

"Maxwell, I do not pay you to question or understand my orders. Simply do as I request, and make sure I have the money no later than next Monday."

"*Harrumph!* Yes, well, whatever you say, sir," muttered Maxwell. "I shall need you to sign these documents, and I'll get on this matter as soon as I return to town."

"See that you do, Maxwell."

Allison heard the scratching sound of pen on paper.

"Thank you, sir. I shall return by Monday. Will that be all, Don Carlos?"

"Hmm? Yes, yes," Don Carlos said in a distracted tone. "I'll let you know if I need anything else."

Allison slipped into the library before the man strode past. She peeked out. He was short and portly, with a glistening bald head. From the dark suit he wore and the topic he and Don Carlos had discussed, Allison guessed he was a lawyer or a banker. She also surmised that the room next door was Don Carlos's den or private office.

Not wanting to run into the man any sooner than necessary, she eased the library door closed and turned to admire the immense room. Its coffered ceilings and rosewood paneling set off by the dark burgundy rug of an ornate Middle Eastern design gave the library a plush, masculine feel. And the books! Two of the walls were lined with shelves of books from floor to ceiling. A rosewood ladder slid along a track at the top of the shelves, inviting readers to browse even the highest shelf in search of the right book.

Allison could never resist books. She slid her hand across the soft leather backs of ancient tomes as if the information contained inside could somehow seep into her fingers through mere touch. She inhaled. The room smelled like a library, a very rich man's library: The strong scent of leather mingled with that old-book smell and a hint of sweet pipe tobacco.

She stepped past shelf after shelf, her hand still caressing the spines of gilded leather covers and her gaze slipping from title to title, when she came to what appeared to be the novels section. Someone in the family seemed to have an interest in science fiction. There were several by Jules Verne and H. G. Wells: *Twenty Thousand Leagues under the Sea, The War of the Worlds, The Time Machine.* Feeling a sense of irony, she pulled *The Time Machine* from the shelf.

Like the others, the book was a leather-bound first edition. Of course, in 1906 that wasn't so very unusual. Most of the classic novels on the shelves couldn't have been more than ten or twenty years old. Allison carried the book to the window seat and slid the heavy drape partway across the window so she was hidden in a small alcove between the glass and the drape. She'd always dreamed of sitting in a quiet luxurious room, tucked behind a curtain, reading on a window seat.

She leaned back against a cushion and opened the book. It was signed by H. G. Wells for María Teresa Cardona Pomales. *Wow!* Allison traced the signature with her finger. So Tere enjoyed science fiction. What would she think if she knew about the time travel happening right under her nose?

Allison turned to the first chapter and began to read. Soon her eyes grew heavy; she could barely keep them open. She lay the book on her lap and closed her eyes. Tere had woken her so early, and she was so tired...

Something caused Allison to slowly open her eyes. She must have fallen asleep because she had not noticed that someone had entered the library and was standing a few feet away, gazing through the French doors at the garden. It was Don Carlos. His hands were locked behind his back, and he was deep in thought. A look of such intense sorrow consumed his features that Allison almost felt sorry for the man.

She wished she hadn't intruded on this private scene. But apparently Don Carlos had not noticed her tucked behind the drape. Forgetting the book on her lap, Allison shrank further into the corner. The book slipped and fell to the carpet with a loud *thud*.

Startled, Don Carlos jumped, his head snapping toward the sound. Allison drew back into the shadow of the drape, but the skirt of her dress and her torso were still visible. The man's eyes narrowed. He took a step forward and froze. His face grew as white as his hair.

"*¡Madre de Dios!*" he whispered, as his gaze took in the ruby-red gown.

"Oh!" Allison gasped, watching his expression.

The man swallowed, still staring at the girl in the shadows. Then, regaining his composure, he ripped open the drape and towered over her, glaring.

"I—I'm sorry," said Allison. "I didn't mean to startle you. I must have fallen asleep and—"

Don Carlos grabbed her arm and yanked her up, forcing her to stand before him like a naughty student before the principal. "What are you doing in that dress?"

Allison fought the urge to cringe at his hostility. She stuck out her chin as she'd seen Tere do. "Tere gave it to me—to wear until I can sew my own."

Don Carlos released her as though she had suddenly turned into a poisonous snake. He stared at her again, his expression turning from one of puzzlement back to one of antagonism. "How dare you call my daughter by her first name!"

"She asked me to!" Allison could feel the sparks flying from her eyes.

Don Carlos turned his back to Allison. "My daughter is often misguided when she thinks with her heart. But a servant should know her place."

"I'm sorry if you are offended, sir, but Miss Teresa has made it perfectly clear I am an employee, not a servant."

Don Carlos whipped around, his steel-blue eyes blazing. "What you are is an insolent child. Did the Thompsons teach you nothing?"

"The Thompsons are dead," Allison replied, "but I'm sure they would have taught me what they could if they'd lived. In the meantime, I've had to figure things out on my own. I think I've done a pretty good job, considering."

Don Carlos's jaw dropped. The strange look of puzzlement returned. He shook his head, as if to clear confusion. When he spoke again, his tone was less harsh.

"What is it my daughter has hired you to do?"

"I'm her seamstress, as you probably know."

Don Carlos nodded.

"I'll sew for the family, and I am to help her care for your wife..."

"A child like you? To assume that type of responsibility? What could Tere have been thinking?" He muttered the last part mainly to himself. Then, as if he suddenly remembered to whom he was speaking, he asked, "What else? Is there more?"

"Well... she wants me to help care for Miss Isabel." Allison released this information reluctantly, somehow sensing that the knowledge would further infuriate the man.

She was right. Don Carlos's face turned the shade of her ruby-red dress. His eyes bulged, his white hair flared.

"I forbid it!" he bellowed. "No one but her sister and her nurse shall care for my Isa, do you understand?"

With those words, he turned on his heel and slammed out of the room.

CHAPTER 21

In the days that followed, Don Carlos seemed to tolerate Allison the way an old cat might tolerate the new household puppy, keeping his distance, but at the same time, keeping a wary eye on the unwelcome addition to his family. Allison was aware of the strange look that passed over his face whenever she crossed his path. But she also noticed that when she stood her ground with him, he was less gruff.

A few days after Allison's encounter with Don Carlos in the library, Tere took the buggy and drove alone to San Francisco. She did this against her father's wishes. At dinner, the night before she left, he had urged that she wait until he was free to go with her. Allison witnessed the quarrel because Tere insisted she eat dinner with the family in the evenings.

"Papá," Tere began, her voice firm and steady, "I cannot wait another week. I have business in the city, and I want to do my spring shopping."

"There is no urgency in spring shopping," he insisted. "It is not safe for you to drive so far alone."

"You do it."

"Tere, Tere, I am a man—"

Tere's head snapped up. "And I am a full-grown woman!"

"But Tere, I must continue to impress on you: There is a difference between men and women and what they should and should not do."

"I have no wish to be ruled by what I should or should not do. I can drive a buggy, ride a horse, and wield a whip better than any man I know."

Don Carlos gave his head a tired shake. "I have no doubt you are a skilled horsewoman—I taught you myself. But San Francisco is a dangerous city. At least take one of the men—I can spare Fernando or Marcelo."

"Papá, I am not going to the Barbary Coast," Tere said, swishing back her chestnut curls. "I shall be staying on Nob Hill with Eda Funston and the General. I see no reason why I need another person—man or woman—to escort me."

Don Carlos threw up his hands in resignation and left the table early, muttering under his breath about the folly of modern young women.

Allison had been holding her breath during the conversation, silently rooting for Tere, hoping she would go to San Francisco a week early so she'd be safe at home when the earthquake struck.

When Don Carlos was safely out of earshot, Tere burst into giggles and winked at Allison. "*Ay,* Bequita, wait until you see what I bring back from San Francisco!"

During the days Tere was still home, Allison learned the routine around the mansion. Since Allison had been prohibited from helping with Isa, midmornings and early afternoons involved entertaining Doña Ana. Tere insisted Allison's visits were beginning to perk up the frail woman, so they became a daily ritual.

Allison had to agree that once Doña Ana understood Allison spoke only English, and she no longer mistook Allison for Isa, she did appear to enjoy Allison's company. There was a glow in her small birdlike eyes, and she sat up in bed more and more often. She also stopped needing Magda's herbs and potions, which seemed to keep her in a sedated, often confused, state.

It concerned Allison, however, that the woman's color was still pale and sallow. "I think she needs sunlight," she remarked to Tere one morning.

"I have no doubt the sun would do her good, but Mamá refuses to let anyone open the drapes."

Allison had been thinking more of direct sunlight and fresh air than merely opening the drapes. But one step at a time. Perhaps if she could convince the woman to allow the sun into her chamber, she could later convince her to venture outside. So on the morning Tere left for San Francisco, Allison marched into Doña Ana's room and threw open the drapes.

Doña Ana gasped and shrank away from the light, covering her face with her hands as if she were a creature of the night, doomed to extermination if once touched by the sun.

"No, no, *niña, por favor,* close the drapes!"

Allison knelt beside the bed and took one of the woman's cold trembling hands in hers. "Doña Ana, please listen to me. The sun will not hurt you. It is good for you—it will make your bones strong and healthy. It will warm your cold hands. Look, see how lovely your room looks washed in warm sunlight. And see what I brought you"—Allison presented her with a vase of fresh roses—"Smell, isn't it delicious?"

Doña Ana peered out from under her comforter. Her wrinkled brow relaxed when she saw the heavenly bouquet of pastel-colored tea roses blended with delicate daisies.

"You did this?"

Allison nodded, smiling. "Come, let me help you sit. I'll hold the vase on your lap while you inhale the sweet fragrance."

Doña Ana allowed Allison to sit her up and place the vase on her lap.

"*Qué olor bello,*" she said, breathing in the scent. "Isa loves roses. I have not had roses in my room since she..." Tears began to shine in Doña Ana's eyes.

"Here, let me pull one out so you can hold it while I read to you," Allison offered, wanting to distract the woman from her sad thoughts. "What would you like me to read today? I brought a book of Emily Dickinson's poems. Shall I read a few?"

"I enjoy the sound of your voice, *mija*. It causes me to think of a whispering angel. Anything you read shall be lovely."

Allison blushed at the compliment, briefly wondering as she began to read whether it was her voice or Becky's that the woman heard.

Each day, Allison encouraged Doña Ana to do a bit more. The first day of Tere's departure, Doña Ana allowed the drapes to remain open the entire morning, ordering them closed just before her afternoon nap. The next day, Allison insisted they be opened in the morning and again in the afternoon, when Doña Ana awoke from her nap. And she propped up the old woman in bed with several pillows behind her back, getting her ready to sit up on her own. She also cracked open the windows, allowing the warm afternoon breeze to bring in the pungent smell of sun-ripening grapes.

On the third day, Allison distracted the woman in such a manner that before she was aware of it, she was sitting on the edge of the bed with her thin legs dangling over the side. At first, Doña Ana complained of dizziness and weakness. But Allison wouldn't allow her to lie back down. Instead, she sat beside her and held her while the dizziness passed, entertaining the woman by telling her stories of animals and forests.

Doña Ana was so pleased with her progress that that afternoon, she allowed Allison and Nelda to carry her to a chair next to the fireplace. There she had a view of the rose garden and the vineyards beyond and at the same time could warm her legs. Allison had run out of animal stories, so she returned to the book of Emily Dickinson's poems to entertain Doña Ana.

"It is a shame you do not speak Spanish, Becky," Doña Ana commented in a whimsical tone. "Spanish lyrics would sound heavenly coming from your lips."

On the fourth day, Allison brazenly threw open the French doors, announcing, "I have a surprise for you, Doña Ana."

At Allison's instruction, Nelda entered, pushing a wooden wheelchair Allison had requested her to find.

"Today, we visit the rose garden," Allison said, wrapping a satin quilted robe around Doña Ana's shoulders.

"But I cannot," Doña Ana protested. "I—"

"Why can't you?" Allison signaled Nelda to bring the chair to the side of the bed. "You sat in a chair for two hours yesterday. What's the difference between sitting in a regular chair and a wheelchair?"

While Doña Ana protested feebly, Allison had Nelda help her lift the woman's light form onto the wheelchair. Allison straightened the robe and tucked it around Doña Ana's ankles.

"There. Now you'll be warm and comfortable," Allison told her. "Let's try five minutes in the sun. After that, if you still want, we'll bring you back in. Right, Nelda?"

The nurse glanced nervously at Allison, whispering, "Don Carlos, what if he—?"

Allison shook her head and nodded meaningfully at Doña Ana. "Shall we go?" she said cheerfully.

Without waiting for either woman to protest further, Allison wheeled the chair through the open doors and onto the stone path to the rose garden. The wheelchair, with its large unsteady wheels, handled awkwardly over the bumpy path. Unlike the sleek, heavy-duty chrome wheelchairs of the nineties, this chair was made of wood and woven rattan, and the wheels were attached to a wrought-iron frame.

She pushed the chair to the other side of the house, where the sun shone brightly and a gentle breeze carried the scent of flowers to the small party of women. Allison picked a partially open rosebud and offered it to Doña Ana.

The woman accepted it graciously and brought it to her nose. As she glanced around the garden, Doña Ana's eyes grew misty. "I have missed this place," she said with a sigh. "I used to come out every morning, tend my roses, and pick a few for Isa's and Tere's rooms. But when Isa grew ill, I refused to indulge in the pleasure—not while my Isa—" She took Allison's hand and squeezed it. "My dear, you have returned to me something very precious. I see now that punishing myself will not bring Isa back to health. It has merely robbed me of mine."

"Would you prefer to go in now, or would you like to stay longer?" Allison asked.

Doña Ana took another moment to gaze about before answering. "It is enough for today. I grow tried. But tomorrow, we shall return. *Gracias, mija,*" she said to Allison. "Thank you for more than I can ever express."

The next day, Tere was due back from San Francisco. It was a warm, cloudless day, and Allison decided to wait until the afternoon to take Doña Ana for her trip to the rose garden.

Once the woman was bundled in her robe, Allison and Nelda wheeled her to the garden. Allison had found an English translation of *Don Quixote de la Mancha* next to a copy of the original Spanish version. Thinking Doña Ana might enjoy a classic novel from her country, even if it were read in English, Allison pulled it from the shelf. When Nelda was settled on a concrete bench, Allison curled on the grass at Doña Ana's feet and began to read.

Doña Ana was pleased. She explained that *Don Quixote* was a family favorite. As a child, Tere begged her mother to read her parts of it. And often in the evening, next to a crackling fire in the drawing room, Don Carlos would read their favorite passages aloud. While Tere identified with Don Quixote fighting windmills, Isa preferred stories about damsels in distress being saved by knights in shining armor. Tere would cuddle against her father, her head on his chest, listening to his rich, deep voice as he read with passion and conviction. But Isa would lie on a sofa, thoroughly bored, except for the parts about the damsel Dulcinea.

Doña Ana seemed a bit like Isa and quickly grew impatient when Allison began reading from the beginning. She instructed Allison as to which chapters to turn to and which passages to read. Never having read *Don Quixote,* Allison would have preferred to read the book as it was intended to be read, but it tickled her that Doña Ana was beginning to take enough interest in things to start issuing orders and to enjoy small pleasures.

As the afternoon wore on and the sun grew warmer, Nelda began to nod, Allison was engrossed in the passage she was reading, and Doña Ana was transported by the soft, clear voice. No one noticed a figure stride silently across the lawn toward the small group of women. Only when a shadow slid over the page Allison was reading did she realize that someone had joined them. She looked up to see Don Carlos looming over her; his expression was one of disbelief, and his eyes held an emotion she could not make out.

"Carlos," said Doña Ana, awakened from her trance by Allison's silence. She smiled, glowing, and held out her small hands. Her husband knelt beside her and brought her hands to his lips.

"How could you...when did this happen?" Don Carlos was obviously pleased by his wife's unexpected progress.

"Isn't it wonderful? We owe it all to this angel of a child." Doña Ana gazed fondly at Allison.

"You mean to say Dr. Guzman has not approved this?" The man's face darkened. "Nelda, how could you have allowed such an excursion?"

"*Lo siento, señor,* but—"

Allison stood and faced the man. "Don't blame Nelda. I insisted that we start bringing Doña Ana into the garden. She needs sunlight and fresh air. It's not healthy to keep her cooped up all the time, never even opening the drapes. The sun is good for her bones—"

"Ah, so you are a doctor now, is that it?" Don Carlos rose to his full height, towering over her.

Allison refused to be intimidated. "It doesn't take a medical degree to see that a person can't thrive in a dungeonlike atmosphere. Look at her! Doña Ana's face is beginning to get some color, and she is beginning to care about life again."

Suddenly, Doña Ana began to laugh, a delighted laugh that rose from deep in her belly. Allison and Don Carlos stopped arguing and looked down at the frail form in the wheelchair.

She covered her mouth as she tried to stop laughing. "The way Becky stands up to you, Carlos"—Doña Ana smothered another giggle—"she reminds me of our Tere."

Don Carlos clenched his jaw. "She is an insolent child! A servant, no less." He glared at Allison. "I would dismiss you on the spot if I didn't think my daughter would simply rehire—"

"*Ah-ooo-gah! Ah-oo-gaaah!*"

Around the bend of the main road to the estate appeared Tere, decked out in a tan overcoat with matching bonnet tied by a scarf beneath her chin. She was driving a brand-new convertible automobile.

CHAPTER 22

"*Madre de Dios!* What in the Virgin Mother's name has that girl done now?" Don Carlos muttered as he watched Tere maneuver the motorcar to a halt at the edge of the lawn.

Tere grinned and waved as if she were riding a float in a parade. She hopped from the car and flew across the lawn, holding up her long skirts and exposing her slender black-stockinged legs. She swooped on them, laughing and panting and tossing her chestnut curls as she unknotted the scarf from under her chin and removed the bonnet.

"Mamá, you look wonderful!" she exclaimed, once she had caught her breath. "This must be a miracle."

Don Carlos snorted, and Doña Ana laughed.

"Perhaps not a miracle," she said, "but it was the work of an angel—your protégée."

"Becky?" Tere spun around in search of Allison, who had retreated to the concrete bench beside Nelda. "Of course, it was. I knew she would be a perfect addition to our household."

"Enough about the confounded girl," Don Carlos snapped. "What is that—that contraption doing here?"

"It is an automobile, Papá," Tere replied with a giggle, "a horseless carriage."

"I know perfectly well what an automobile is! I'm not a bumbling idiot! I want to know what you are doing driving it."

"I bought it. I ordered it last fall when we went to the city for our Christmas shopping. The man told me it would probably arrive in late March or early April. When I picked it up, he gave me four hours of driving instructions and sent me on my way. Isn't it beautiful? Mamá, perhaps when you are feeling stronger, I will take you—"

"You *bought* it?" Don Carlos had been staring at his daughter openmouthed since she announced the car's purchase. "With whose money, may I ask?"

"My trust fund. Abuelita left no instructions on how I should use it, so I—"

"So you frittered away your grandmother's trust fund on a passing fancy? Teresa, I thought you had more sense."

"I frittered away nothing. I purchased it with part of my annual income. Anyway, Papá, a motorcar is not a passing fancy. It is a thing of the future, and, after all, this is the twentieth century."

"Thing of the future, indeed! If you had been a good and docile child, you would be married by now and some other man's headache." Don Carlos began to walk away, shaking his head, when he turned back, and said, "What have you done with my buggy? Teresa, if you have sold my good buggy to help pay for that—"

"Do not worry, Papá. Your buggy is safe. I hired a

man to drive it back for me. He should arrive sometime tonight."

"A man? You gave my good horse and buggy to some stranger? Why did you not simply stand in the middle of Market Street and hand out the family fortune to passing beggars?"

"Honestly, Papá, you act as if I were a child. I did not simply hand over your horse and buggy without security. We struck a bargain. The man needed a ride to this part of the country, and I needed someone to drive the buggy home. I lent him the buggy in exchange for this beautiful chain and cross."

Tere opened her overcoat and displayed a heavy gold rope around her neck at the end of which hung a gold cross. The cross was about two inches long and studded with six large rubies.

At the sight of the cross, Doña Ana gasped and slumped back in a dead faint.

"Ana will be fine, Carlos. She simply had too much excitement for one day. After years confined to her bed, her body is not used to so much activity at once. She needs some rest."

Allison and Tere stood silently in the shadows, just inside Doña Ana's bedroom door, and listened anxiously to what Dr. Guzman told Don Carlos.

"So she should not be allowed out of bed again?"

"On the contrary, Carlos," Dr. Guzman replied. "It was never my intention that Ana become an invalid. It was *she* who shrank from the world, denying herself even the simplest pleasures. I could not even convince her to open the drapes. She claimed it hurt her eyes and brought her pain, remembering... No, I fully support whoever was able to draw her from her self-imposed prison."

Tere squeezed Allison's shoulder and whispered in her ear, "Did you hear, Bequita? Isn't it wonderful?"

"What else should we do, Alejandro?" said Don Carlos. "Are you leaving any medicine?"

"No, no more medicine. And stop giving her Magda's concoctions. Tomorrow morning have Nelda open up the drapes and let in some air. As soon as Ana is up to it, take her back to the rose garden. But do not overdo."

Don Carlos threw Allison a veiled glance. Tere caught it and squeezed her hand supportively. They both knew the first battle had been won: Don Carlos would no longer stand in their way with respect to Doña Ana. Allison wondered if she would have time to win one for Isa.

"He's here, Allison," Joshua whispered as he led her from her balcony and into the rose garden that evening. "I saw him!"

"Who's here? What are you so excited about?"

"The man—the shaggy man who chases you in the woods. I was alone in the stable, getting the horses ready for the night, when he drove up in Don Carlos's buggy."

"So he's the one Tere hired to bring the buggy back," Allison murmured. "Are you sure he's the right man?"

"I can only go by what you told me, but he seems to fit the description. Shaggy black hair and beard, ragged clothes, real sunburned. Looks like a hermit."

"Sounds like him. Did you talk to him—ask him who he is?"

Joshua nodded. "A little, but he's real skittish, not much of a talker. Asked me to let Miz Teresa know that the buggy had arrived and that she could keep the cross as payment for use of the buggy. He would be honored if she would wear it often."

"He let her keep the cross? That's strange. It looked awfully valuable. I'll bet he could sell it for a lot of money."

"He is peculiar at that. He looked tired and hungry, so I asked him if he wanted some food. He glanced around, kinda nervouslike—reminded me of a hunted rabbit. Then he thanked me and said no, he had food in his bag. But I could tell he was tempted, so I offered to let him sleep in the stable. He just shook his head, grabbed his bundle, and left."

"He's gone!"

"Sorry, Allison. What was I supposed to do? I couldn't force him to stay."

"No, I guess not. But I didn't even get to look at him, to see whether or not he's the right guy. And we don't know anything about him. We don't even know for sure if he's dangerous."

"I know a couple of things about him. He's honest. He could've kept the horse and buggy, but instead he brings them home and doesn't even expect payment for his effort. Even gives away the one thing of value he owns to a woman he's just met."

Allison considered Joshua's comment. "Those sure don't seem like the actions of a murderer. But you said you knew a couple of things about him. What's the second?"

"He's a Spaniard. I could tell by his accent."

The next day, Doña Ana seemed agitated and distraught. She begged to be left alone with the drapes closed. But once Tere had seen the progress her mother had made, she refused to give in to the woman's whims and allow her to regress to her former invalid state. She drew the drapes and cracked open the windows. And she had Allison bring in several vases of fresh flowers. Then they sat with her and tried to make interesting conversation. But all their efforts couldn't seem to distract Doña Ana from her state of distress.

Doña Ana kept staring at the cross around Tere's neck. Tere had been pleased when Joshua gave her the news that the man had allowed her to keep the cross. She displayed it prominently against her chest.

At one point, Doña Ana said, "Tere, tell me about this man—the man who gave you the cross."

"There is nothing to tell, Mamá. He seems like a sad man. I doubt he has a nickel to his name, and yet he was generous enough to allow me to keep this beautiful chain and cross." Tere fingered the cross, holding it so the sun sparkled off the rubies, casting brilliant red reflections on the walls.

"Describe him to me."

"Why are you so curious, Mamá? He is simply a stranger."

"Humor me, *mija,*" insisted Doña Ana. "Tell me what he looks like."

"Of course, if you wish. He told me he is a sailor and recently arrived in San Francisco from the coast of India. He looked like a sailor, skin tough and darkened by the sun, long black hair and beard, and quite ragged."

"A sailor?" Doña Ana appeared pleased with the news. The tension seemed to lift from her face. "And ragged, you say?"

Tere chuckled. "Papá would definitely not approve of such an acquaintance, even if he is a Spaniard."

"A Spaniard?" Doña Ana leaned toward Tere. "Did he say how a poor sailor acquired such a valuable piece of jewelry?"

Tere thought for a moment. "Come to think of it, he did mention it was given to him by a very dear friend. Oh, I truly must find him and repay him. This is too generous a gift."

"Tere, listen to me," said Doña Ana. "Did this man tell you his name?"

"Only that they call him El León. Why all the questions, Mamá?"

"Tere, this cross is an heirloom from my mother's side of the family. Your father is not familiar with it, and unbeknownst to him, I gave it to Isa when she turned seventeen. The last time I saw it was just before she eloped with José."

CHAPTER 23

That afternoon, when Allison and Tere met at Doña Ana's bedroom, they were surprised to find the woman bright and alert and sitting up in bed.

"Mamá, you must be feeling better," said Tere. "Are you ready for a trip to the garden?"

"*Sí, hija,* I would like to take a trip, but not to the rose garden."

"Not in my automobile, I hope!" Tere laughed. "Papá would never forgive me for taking you for a ride in the motorcar before you were strong enough."

"Your *papá* would not be happy about where I want to go now, either. But he is not home, so he shall never know. He told me he would be gone most of the afternoon. But he will be back in plenty of time for dinner, so we must hurry."

"*Está bien,* Mamá; but you have not yet told me where you wish to go."

"I want to see Isa. Take me to her."

"Mamá—"

"Tere, do not argue with me. This is important. Help

me into the chair. You and Becky shall take me. We'll tell Nelda only that I want to tour the house."

Allison and Tere helped the woman into her wheelchair and wrapped a light blanket around her legs. While Allison pushed the wheelchair, Tere spoke to Nelda.

As they neared the west wing, Doña Ana gave her daughter further instructions: "Tere, run ahead and send Socorro on an errand. Becky and I shall wait here. As soon as Socorro is gone, come back and open the gate for us. I do not want to take any chances that the nurses will inadvertently say something to your father."

Looking puzzled, Tere did as she was told. Several minutes later, she returned and led Allison and Doña Ana through the wrought-iron gates to Isa's bedroom door.

Before Tere could open the door, Doña Ana said, "Remove the cross, Tere, and put it in your pocket. I do not want to upset Isa by letting her see it. How is she, today?"

"Socorro said she's about the same. A bit more agitated, maybe."

Doña Ana nodded sadly, her eyes moist. "All these years and nothing has changed." She took a deep breath and ran her fingers over her hair, smoothing her silver curls. "Hurry, Tere, take me in or I may lose my courage."

Tere unlocked the door and stepped aside so Allison could wheel in the chair. Tere had begun to lock Isa's bedroom door in addition to the iron gate since they had discovered how Isa had escaped the week before: She had snuck from her room while Socorro was napping and had found a loose window in an adjoining room. Until then, she had been allowed to wander the west wing.

Isa was sitting in a rocker in front of barred glass

doors, gazing out at the garden and humming to the baby doll on her lap. Her golden-red hair was more disheveled than the last time Allison had seen her; strands leaped from her head, wild and electric. She did not acknowledge their presence.

Tere motioned for Allison to place the wheelchair in the middle of the room. Then she knelt beside her sister.

"Isa," she said, placing a hand on her shoulder. Isa jumped, startled, but continued to stare out the window. "Isa, I have a surprise for you. Look, you have company. Someone you haven't seen in a very long time."

Isa stopped rocking. "Company? Is it José? Has my dear José come back for me?" She began to straighten her dress and fuss with her hair. "How do I look, Tere? Help me with my hair. I need to look nice for José."

Tere pushed a few stray strands from Isa's face. "You look beautiful, Isa. But—"

Isa stood, dropping the doll from her lap, and turned. Her eyes scanned the room. "José? Where are you?"

"Isa, *mi amor*..." Doña Ana held out her arms to her elder daughter.

Apparently noticing her mother for the first time, Isa ran to her and knelt at her feet. "Mamá, have you seen José? He promised he would come back for me. I have been waiting."

"No, mi angel," Doña Ana said, smoothing Isa's tangled curls. "I have not seen José in a very long time."

"He is coming, Mamá, I know he is. But"—Isa glanced around suspiciously—"we must not let Papá know. Promise me, Mamá. You will never tell him José is coming." Isa looked up into her mother's eyes. "Promise me."

Doña Ana winced. "I promise, Isa. If José ever comes back—"

"He will, Mamá, he will. You may doubt him, but I do not. I know he is coming."

"How do you know, *mija*? Tell me."

"Because he promised me. José would never break a promise to me. He loves me. And because I feel it here—" Isa placed her hand over her heart. "I know it is time."

Doña Ana took Isa's face in her hands and spoke softly and slowly, as though she were speaking to a child of three. "Isa, listen carefully. Do you remember the ruby cross I gave you on your seventeenth birthday?"

Isa's hand flew up to her neck, feeling for the cross. Her eyes gazed past her mother. "Abuelita's cross?" She nodded, still staring at something only she could see. She made a motion with her hands, as if she were taking something from her neck and lifting it over her head. She held out her hands, waiting for someone to take the imaginary item.

"Joselito, take this cross as my wedding gift to you. Wear it always, and it will keep you safe. If we are ever parted, I shall know you are coming for me when you return the cross to me by messenger. Let it serve as our secret signal."

Doña Ana's face turned pale; she closed her eyes. Allison heard Tere's quick intake of breath as she digested the information.

"Isa"—Doña Ana took Isa's hand in hers—"you gave the cross to José?"

Slowly, Isa brought her gaze down until it was resting on her mother's face. Her expression was one of pure joy. "José is coming for me, Mamá."

"Isa, *mija,* think carefully. Did José send you the cross while you were at the convent?"

Isa's eyes again stared past her mother. Her beatific smile faded, replaced by an anguished grimace. "Something is wrong," she said in a chilling whisper. "José must be hurt. Otherwise he would have sent me the cross." Isa rose, towering over the small woman in the wheelchair. "Papá must have found out about our plan. He must have stopped him or—"

Isa glared down at her mother. Her face held a mixture of pain and disbelief. "You were the only one I told, other than Magda, the only one I trusted. You told him, didn't you? You told Papá, José was coming for me at the convent. That was why José never sent me the final message—the cross—because Papá stopped him. And it was your fault!"

Isa reached down and gave the wheelchair a mighty shove, sending Doña Ana speeding across the bare tiled floor. Allison, who had been standing against a wall where she could watch but remain in the background, leaped for the wheelchair, barely stopping it from hitting the wall. She caught Doña Ana in her arms as the woman flopped forward.

Doña Ana shook uncontrollably, sobbing and hiding her face in trembling hands. "*Perdóname,* Isa, I am so sorry. I never thought—"

"How could you, Mamá? I hate you!" Isa screamed, lunging at her mother with clenched fists. Her hair flew out in plumes and swirled about her head, accentuating the rage that consumed her face and blazed in her eyes.

Tere stepped between Isa and her mother. She trapped Isa's arms at her sides with her own.

As Isa struggled to free herself from Tere's strong grasp, she continued to scream at her mother. "If something horrible happened to José, it was your fault! Everything was your fault. If I could have escaped with José, I'd still have my baby. But because of you, I lost José, and I lost my precious baby! I'll never forgive you, Mamá, never!"

In a great burst of energy, Isa ripped her arms free from Tere's grasp. She made another attempt to grab Doña Ana, but Tere tackled her from behind and threw her to the floor.

"Get Mamá out of here, Becky, go!" Tere yelled as she wrestled with her sister, who squirmed beneath her like an angry alligator.

As the sisters thrashed about on the slippery tiles, Allison tried to guide the wheelchair past them. She had almost reached the door when a blood-chilling scream froze her feet to the floor.

"José!" Isa cried between hysterical laughs and sobs. "José is coming! *¡Gracias a Dios!* He is alive!"

Allison spun around to see Isa lying on her back with Tere sprawled on top of her. Isa had ceased struggling, and from her hand dangled the golden chain and ruby-studded cross.

CHAPTER 24

Isa's cross!" Magda said, gazing at the rubies as they caught the firelight and reflected it back in crimson flashes.

Magda hadn't been surprised to see Allison and Joshua march into her little cottage in the late afternoon. In fact, she had been expecting them. Another of her premonitions. She had even set the table for tea. What she wasn't expecting was to see Allison wearing the ruby cross.

"You've seen it before?" asked Allison.

Magda nodded. "The night Isa eloped with my brother, they came here first. Isa was wearing it. It was the first and last time I ever saw it, but I never forgot it. After Isa came back from the convent, Doña Ana asked me whether I had ever seen Isa wearing it. Apparently Isa had lost it. Wherever did you find it?"

"It's a long story," Allison replied. "Better sit while I tell you."

Magda poured the sarsaparilla tea while Allison recounted the story, starting with Tere's arrival in the automobile and ending with Isa's finding the ruby cross. "It fell from Tere's pocket while they were thrashing about on the floor."

When Allison finished her story, Magda sat quietly staring into the fire, watching its flaming tongues stretch to lick the kettle. "Isa gave the cross to my brother. If its return is a message, he may truly be alive."

"But to find him," said Allison, "we first have to find that man—the one who calls himself El León."

"*Sí,*" whispered Magda, "we must find El León." She grew quiet again, still staring into the fire. Then she said, "How is Isa?"

"Tere gave her one of your potions to make her sleep. Once she was asleep, Tere took the cross from Isa's hand. Socorro's watching over her now."

"I will send some different herbs back with you—for Isa. I also dried a new batch of peppermint and chamomile. Doña Ana might enjoy some teas to help settle her nerves."

"Nothing too strong for Doña Ana, though. She's been doing better since she's been more... lucid." Allison shook her head. "Poor Doña Ana. All these years she's been living with the guilt of what her betrayal of Isa's confidence has done to Isa. And now, to have her daughter accuse her of being the cause of her misfortune. What a horrible burden."

"It's a real shame it happened when she was starting to perk up," said Joshua.

"She's actually holding up pretty well, considering. She's putting up a brave front so Don Carlos won't ask questions. Doña Ana doesn't want him to find out about the cross or her visit to Isa. She's insisting that this time, no one must betray Isa's confidence. If José really is out there somewhere, Doña Ana wants Isa to be able to see him. She's convinced it's the only thing that will make her well."

Allison lifted the golden rope over her head. "I need to be getting back to the estate. Tere wanted me to bring you the ruby cross for safekeeping. And we were thinking—" Allison shot a look at Joshua.

"You think you could hold it, Magda?" said Joshua, picking up on Allison's signal. "We thought you might be able to see something about José and this man El León."

Magda took the chain and cross in both hands, holding them in front of her as Isa had done when she was holding the imaginary cross. Then she drew her hands to her chest and closed her eyes.

Joshua moved to Allison's side and squeezed her hand as they watched. For a few minutes, nothing happened. Then Magda began to sway and moan, clutching the cross to her chest, in her fists. Suddenly, Magda screamed in agony and threw the cross from her hands. She rolled up into herself and fell to the floor in a heap.

"Magda!" Joshua lifted the woman's head onto his lap. She was unconscious. "Allison, here, take my place. Hold her head like this. She's fainted and I have to find one of her vials..."

Allison took Joshua's place while he jumped to one of Magda's wall cupboards and pulled out a tiny red vial. Popping open the top, he placed the vial under Magda's nose. Magda moaned and began to stir. She tossed her head from side to side, grimacing at the smell.

Allison said softly, "Are you all right?"

Slowly, Magda opened her eyes. When she saw Allison, her face twisted with pain.

"What did you see, Magda?" said Joshua. "Can you tell us?"

She closed her eyes again. "Pain, in my head, pounding. Something hit me on the head. No—not me, it was José. Arms tied behind him, legs bound. Boots kicking him in the ribs, in the stomach. Pain, so much pain. Someone is lifting him, carrying him, shoving him down. A ship, swaying, nausea—awful nausea. Thirsty, so thirsty. Smells, stench, horrible. Can't move...so much pain."

Magda cried out at the memory. She curled back into a ball, pulling away from Allison and moaning.

"Magda?" Allison said, touching her shoulder.

Joshua pulled Allison away. "Shhhh, let her rest. She needs to move through the pain."

While they waited for Magda to recover, Allison sat at the table, warming her chilled hands on the ceramic mug of tea, and Joshua paced the floor. At last, Magda ceased moaning and, with obvious effort, pulled herself to a sitting position on the floor. Joshua and Allison waited impatiently for Magda to break her silence.

Slowly, the woman moved to the rocker and wrapped a shawl around her shoulders. She rocked quietly for a few minutes. The only sound in the cottage was the crackling and spitting of the fire and the creaking of a loose board beneath the rocking chair.

Magda took a deep breath and began her story. "I saw what happened to my brother all those years ago. The night José was riding to the convent to take Isa away with him, he was ambushed. I could not see the men's faces. I doubt José ever saw them, either. They beat and bound him. They took him to a ship and held him prisoner until they were well out to sea. Then he was forced to work as a sailor."

"Your brother was shanghaied?" Joshua looked appalled. "No wonder he never showed up at the convent."

"He became very ill but recovered, and spent many years on the ocean, sailing from port to port. Then he was shipwrecked and stranded for years on a small island . . ."

Allison stooped to pick up the ruby cross that still lay where Magda had thrown it. "Do you suppose he met El León aboard a ship? Maybe they became friends, and he asked El León to bring the cross to Isa."

Magda pulled the shawl tighter, as if she couldn't get warm enough. "No, José is not El León's friend," she said in a strange voice. "José *is* El León."

"I can't believe it," said Allison, as Joshua walked her back to the estate. Dusk had settled, and night was descending like a heavy blanket. A few birds still chattered, scolding the unwelcome pair for disrupting their rest. "The man who chases me—or Becky, rather—is Magda's long-lost brother."

"I just don't get it," said Joshua, wagging his head. "Why would he want to hurt Becky?"

"Maybe he doesn't want to hurt Becky. Maybe he only wants to talk to her. He kept yelling, 'Stop, girl,' but Becky panicked. And she had me panicked. I wasn't thinking straight that night. Becky was screaming in my head. I had just stumbled over a dead body and was covered with blood. And someone was definitely chasing me. Then I saw that wild-eyed, shaggy man."

"I don't blame you for getting spooked, Allison. José—if that was him—does look pretty frightful. I was uneasy with him, myself."

"I just can't imagine that the man Magda talks about with such tenderness, the same man Isa loves so passionately, could have turned into such a horrible person."

Joshua gave Allison a hand as she stepped over a log, lifting her long skirts out of the way so she could see where she placed her foot. "It's been years," he reminded her. "People change, Allison. Remember he was shanghaied. Years of living with cutthroats and thugs can turn even the gentlest man into a ruffian. And don't forget, he was shipwrecked, too."

"I guess you have to harden to survive that kind of life. Still, it's sad to think that the man Isa has waited so many years for could be a murderer."

"Remember, Allison, we don't know if Sadie's death *is* a murder—could be an accident. You said so yourself. We also don't know if it's José's doing."

"That's true. And he's not our only suspect. He's just the only person I know for sure had the opportunity, because I saw him at the scene. But what's his motive?"

Joshua shook his head. "That's a puzzler. After all these years, I would think he wouldn't even remember Sadie. She was a seamstress at the estate when José disappeared."

"And he arrives only a few days before her death. It doesn't give Sadie a lot of time to make a new enemy."

"But don't forget," said Joshua, "Don Carlos has blackmail as a motive. What if Don Carlos decides not to pay her off after all? What if he decides to finish her off, instead?"

Allison sighed. "I don't know, Joshua. I've gotten to know him a bit better. He's crusty and arrogant and generally dictatorial, but I've seen him with Tere. He softens like clay in a warm hand when he's around her. As nasty as he was with Sadie that night, I can't imagine him committing murder. Especially when he's got the money to pay her off."

"Don't be too sure, Allison. Magda believes he can be ruthless. She used to believe he was responsible for José's disappearance. He'll stop at nothing if he thinks what he's doing is best for his family."

CHAPTER 25

Joshua," Allison said as they ate lunch under the ancient oak, "it's already April sixteenth. We have to find José. We need to know why he wants to talk to Becky, and, more importantly, we have to find out what he knows about Sadie and whether he has a reason to kill her. Because if he doesn't, someone out there does, and we have less than two days to stop him."

"Maybe José will contact Magda soon."

"Not soon enough," Allison replied between bites. "Last time, I first met Magda the evening of the seventeenth—tomorrow night. She had no idea where José was. She said she hadn't heard from him for years."

"But things are different this time. Now Magda knows José is alive and that he's back."

Allison stopped eating and stared at Joshua, taking in what he'd just said. "You're right. Oh, Joshua, you're so right!" Allison clapped her hands to her face in disbelief. "Do you know what this means?"

Joshua opened his mouth to speak, but Allison answered her own question. "It's the first sign of change. It's a sign of hope for all of us that maybe what I'm doing is working. Because I came to work for Tere and helped Doña Ana start living again, she was able to reach out to Isa when the time came. If she hadn't done that, Isa wouldn't have struggled with Tere, and she wouldn't have found the ruby cross, and Magda wouldn't have found out her brother is still alive. And maybe, because I insisted that Tere come back from San Francisco before the eighteenth, José arrived in the buggy earlier than he did the last time." Allison thought about that for a moment. This time when she spoke, her voice was filled with awe. "Joshua, I may be changing history—I may be able to save you and Becky."

Joshua said nothing. He simply gazed at the vineyards beyond. A look that Allison couldn't read had stilled the playful grin and brought the barest frown to his face.

"Joshua?" she said. "What is it?"

He shook his head. "I don't know why I trust you so. You compare what's happening now to a time I've never lived through. You talk about signs and hope. But all I've got is your word that anything bad ever happened before or that anything bad might happen to Becky and me tomorrow or the next day..."

Allison felt as though she had been kicked in the stomach. She managed to speak, using all her willpower to keep her emotions under control. "Joshua, you can't start doubting me now—not now that we're so close to succeeding. I couldn't bear it if—" The words caught in her throat. The thought of having to start convincing him all over again was too much.

"If I could remember... Isn't there something you can tell me to help me believe?"

"You can't remember what hasn't happened. Faith and trust, that's all I can offer. You have to have faith in me and trust that what I tell you is the truth. Whether you believe I'm a very confused Becky or a girl named Allison who comes from a time far from yours, in your gut, you must feel that something unusual has happened." Allison took his hand in hers. "Trust your feelings for Becky"—Allison looked down—"if not for me."

Joshua pulled back his hand and stood, staring again at the vineyards. "That's the problem, Allison. I do care for you. Maybe if I didn't believe this crazy story of yours, things would go back to being simple. I'd only have feelings for Becky, and I wouldn't be faced with having my heart pulled in two directions. I've always been true and loyal to Becky, but now..."

Joshua knelt beside Allison. "Now, whenever I look at your face, I no longer see Becky's face. I see the image of another girl. A girl who's strong and caring and smart as a whip. She has eyes that snap like pinesap in fire and a will of iron. And if what you say is true, in less than two days that girl will leave my life forever, and with her she'll take the sweet, innocent love I had for my Becky. So maybe I don't want to believe."

It wasn't until that moment that Allison realized what she had done to Joshua. She had cared for him since the first moment she saw him in the meadow, his laughing eyes and teasing smile. Maybe she was even in love with him—if you could fall in love in so short a time. But she had been selfish. She had wanted him to like her so badly that she had achieved it, but at what cost? She and Joshua could never be together, and his love for the one girl he'd ever cared for could no longer be pure and undivided. She had to make it up to him. Maybe once history was changed, and he and Becky had survived the earthquake, he'd forget about her, as if she'd never existed.

"Joshua," she said, "this is your time—yours and Becky's. I had no right to intrude. Becky sent me here to save you, not to steal your heart. But perhaps we feel so strongly about each other because somewhere, sometime, you and I are meant to have a chance to be together. In the meantime, you must trust me and believe—"

"Allison?" a woman's voice whispered in her ear. "Sweetheart, can you hear me?"

A gust of cold air seemed to pass through her. Allison hugged her shoulders. "No... not yet. It's too soon."

"Allison?" Joshua said, taking her arms. "You all right? You look like you're going to faint."

Joshua's voice seemed far away and garbled, as if he were speaking from the bottom of a bottle.

"Joshua, I can barely hear you!"

"I'm here, Allison, I'm here."

Allison could tell Joshua was holding her close, but she could no longer feel his arms. It was as though her body had been injected with Novocain. She felt only a fuzzy, cottonlike sensation in her brain and a whirling in her head as if she were going to pass out.

The next moment, she was floating above Joshua as he held Becky's limp body in his arms.

The wind tunnel sucks me from the past and hurls me into the future. I stop struggling, knowing now how useless it is to fight the strong force that propels me.

This must really be a nightmare! Hadn't I just been thinking about how horrible it would be to have to again convince Joshua of the truth? Hadn't I just been thinking about how close we were to succeeding? How many more times will I have to endure this?

"Allison?" Mom whispers. "I have to tell you something, sweetheart. Please try to listen."

I peer through a hazy fog and see Mom sitting beside my hospital bed. I'm floating above the scene, and as I concentrate, the images become more clear, as though the fog is evaporating.

"Sweetheart," Mom says, "in just a few hours, you're going into surgery. The doctor has to drain the hematoma. You're going to be just fine if you fight. Do you hear me, Allison? You need to fight to pull through. I know you can do it, darling, you're the strongest person I know. Fight, Allison, please fight!"

"Allison," Becky whispers, "did you hear what your ma said?"

Yes, surgery.

"Your ma's been frettin'. It seems dangerous."

Becky, what am I doing back here so soon? I had two more days... I was so close...

"I—I'm starting to weaken, Allison. I had to call you back."

But I didn't finish, and now that I'm back here, I don't know if I ever will finish. It may all have been for nothing.

"You might die in surgery." Becky's voice trembles.

And if I come out of the coma too soon, I can't help you any longer. We don't have time to waste. I have to go back. You might never find someone else to take my place.

"I can risk that, but I can't risk your life. You have to stay, Allison. I don't know if I can fight for you."

You have to fight for me. I'm fighting for you!

"But I don't know if I'm strong enough..."

Becky, you have more strength than you realize. You stuck around for decades waiting for someone to help you and Joshua. You fought death.

"And I lost," she says with a whimper.

But you didn't give up. Death won the battle but not the war. Death hasn't won yet. Together we can win. We have to try.

"Twice, Allison," Becky says in a small, frightened voice, "we have to fight and beat death twice—once for me, and once for you. I don't know if I can do it."

You're wrong, Becky—three times. We're fighting for Joshua, too. His life is in our hands. If we give up, he's dead forever. And I can't stay here and fight for my life knowing it was costing two other lives. Even if I won, I wouldn't have much of a life with two deaths on my conscience.

Becky gives out a muffled cry but says nothing.

I don't have a choice, Becky. And neither have you.

I look down at Mom. I can't help but remember how much I always took her for granted, how I didn't appreciate the little things she did for me. Instead, I found them annoying, like she was always hovering. The last morning we spent together, the morning of the accident, I was so distracted, so into myself, I didn't pay any attention to her. I didn't even hug her good-bye.

I promise, Mom, I promise if I ever get out of this and back to you, I'll never take you for granted again. Not ever.

My heart bursts with an immense longing to be held by her. I need to feel her touch, to smell the rosy scent of her perfume. I know that just being held by my mother once more will give me the strength I need to return to the past and face whatever is waiting for me. And the courage to risk never returning to my own life.

Let me in, Becky. Let me be with Mom for a few minutes. Then let me go. And don't call me back until I've finished.

PART FOUR

The Truth

The past dissolves into the now.
I take a chance. Will fate allow
the two of us to meet again?
But oh, if so—no matter when—
your love, I shall extol!

CHAPTER 26

A deafening roar thundered in Allison's ears; the scent of pine and smoke and moist earth overwhelmed her senses. She felt the heaviness of sleep begin to lift as she stretched her quivering limbs.

"Sleeping Beauty awakes on her own."

Slowly, Allison opened her eyes. A smile that made her heart lurch and gray eyes that twinkled in the sunlight were the first things she saw. Joshua was squatting at her side, his attention focused fully on her. His eyes spoke of a joke he was dying to tell.

"Don't you know you're supposed to let the handsome prince kiss you awake?"

"Shall I go back to sleep, and we can try again?"

"Oh, no you don't," Joshua said. "Now that I've got you back, I'm not letting you get away so quick."

"Back?" Allison suddenly realized he might mean getting Becky back after an absence of almost three weeks.

"You've been asleep most the afternoon. The problem with Sleeping Beauty is that she's pretty to look at but not much fun."

"Oh," Allison said, laughing. "I'll try to stay awake."

She let Joshua help her sit up, noticing for the first time that they were at the waterfall pool. Reluctantly, she looked down at her dress, dreading the sight of the faded calico. She sighed with relief when she saw instead the emerald-green gown. Things hadn't changed back to how they were before April first. Joshua still remembered her.

"Becky?" he said. "Are you all right?"

A cold hand clamped around Allison's heart. She felt the blood drain from her face. He didn't remember.

Joshua wrapped his arms around her. "Becky, what's wrong? You look like you're going to faint."

Déjà vu. Weren't those the last words she'd heard him utter only a few hours earlier? Had he forgotten everything? Would she have to start convincing him all over?

"Talk to me. Are you feeling all right?"

"What"—Allison paused to swallow—"what did you call me?"

Joshua loosened his grip on her shoulders. He stared into her eyes, searching deeply, as though he were seeking her soul.

"Allison?" he whispered.

She let out the breath she had been holding, and like a dam collapsing, her emotions spewed forth. She grabbed him in a fierce hug, sobbing loudly in his ear.

"Whoa, whoa, girl. What's going on?"

"Joshua! Oh, Joshua, you remember me!"

"Shhhh, hush now. Of course, I remember you. I just didn't know... when you went to sleep you were Becky."

Allison stopped sobbing and stepped back, so she could study his face. "Becky was here? She came back?"

"When you fainted this morning—"

"This morning? Was that the last time you spoke to me?"

He nodded. "First, we're having lunch at the estate, and the next thing I know, you're turning pale and falling limp into my arms."

"So I've only lost a few hours." Allison was barely able to contain her excitement. "What's today, Joshua? Is it still April sixteenth?"

Joshua nodded.

"In 1906?"

"Of course, it's 1906. And yes, you've only been gone for most of the afternoon."

"Oh, that's wonderful, Joshua, just wonderful! I was so afraid—oh, never mind, it didn't happen." Then something occurred to her. She bit her lower lip. "What did happen when I was gone...when Becky was here?"

Joshua sat back. "I panicked at first. I never had a girl faint in my arms for no reason. And it just doesn't seem like the kind of thing you would do, so I thought you were real sick or something. I laid you back on the bench and put a wet napkin on your head. I was about to run for help, when you started coming around." Joshua gave Allison a quick sideways glance. "But it wasn't you.

"I didn't know that right off, though. I held the wet napkin on her forehead till she felt strong enough, then I helped her sit up. When she looked down at the green dress and shoes she was wearing, she started screaming. I quieted her down right fast, and as soon as I realized she was Becky and not you, I brought her out here. Miz Teresa is probably worried to tears wondering where you are, but I couldn't risk letting her near Becky. Not in the state Becky was in."

"Probably a good idea." Allison wondered how she was going to explain her disappearance to Tere. "Then what? Did you tell her about me?"

A guilty look crossed Joshua's face. He looked down at his hands. "Tell her what about you?"

"Well, that I was here."

Joshua shook his head. "She was in a real bad way. She was shaking and scared and crying, wondering how she got to the estate and into new clothes and a pair of shoes. She hasn't worn shoes since her pa died. Sadie wouldn't spend the money."

"But you told her something. You explained about the dress, didn't you?"

"I asked her what was the last thing she remembered. She said being in the meadow, heading toward the woods to meet me at the waterfall. I asked her the date, and she said it was April first. I told her she must have had one of her blackouts. A long one this time because today was April sixteenth. I figured I better prepare her, since I didn't know if you were ever…" His voice trailed off.

"Ever coming back?" Allison couldn't help wondering if he had hoped she would never come back.

Joshua nodded, glancing up at her. As if he had read her mind, he said, "I wanted you to, but it made me feel so disloyal to Becky."

Allison exhaled slowly and gave him a sad smile. "I understand. So how did she take it when you told her she'd blacked out for over two weeks?"

"She got kind of still and quiet. It spooked me more than when she was crying and carrying on. Then she said her head hurt and she needed to rest her eyes. That's when she fell asleep. I never did get to tell her about how she's living at the estate now and doesn't have to see Sadie anymore."

"Maybe it's best that way," Allison said. "She'll find out soon enough, if everything turns out okay. If not, I guess it doesn't matter."

They decided to spend the rest of the afternoon together. Allison already had to make up some explanation for Tere regarding her absence, and it might be the last time she and Joshua had to be alone together.

Allison took off her shoes and stockings and dangled her feet in the pool as she sat on a wide, flat boulder. Joshua handed her a fishing pole and plunked down beside her with his.

As they fished, they talked about their plans for the next day. Allison would make some excuse, and they would leave the mansion after lunch and head for the Thompson cabin. Since the only thing she knew for sure was that Don Carlos would be there sometime on the afternoon of April seventeenth, they wanted to arrive early. With any luck, Sadie or Don Carlos would mention the subject of the blackmail.

They still had no information on José's whereabouts, but maybe tomorrow would bring news.

Then they talked about themselves. Allison told Joshua about her mom and her friend Jenny and how she missed her dad. Joshua shared what he remembered about his parents, and he told her more about Magda and how good she had been to him.

"Why does Magda limp?" Allison asked.

"It happened when her father was killed in the fire on the estate. She ran into the barn to try to help him, and a burning beam fell on her, crushing her leg and burning it real bad. Dr. Guzman hadn't moved here yet, so José and her mother did the doctorin'. I always thought if we'd had a good doctor nearby, she might not be so crippled."

"Is that why you want to be a doctor?"

"One reason. The other is... I don't know, exactly. It's like a strong pull, a calling maybe. Something I can't control but I want real bad."

"Then you've got to do it, Joshua. You've got to follow your heart."

"It seems so impossible right now. I don't have the money—"

"Remember what I told you, Joshua; there may be scholarships." Allison thought of something and giggled. "And later on, when you're older, I can help you get rich. You could start a clinic or something."

Joshua snorted. "Rich? Me? How can I do that?"

Allison bit her lip. Should she tell him? Why not? He might as well profit from her knowledge. "The stock market. It's going to crash in 1929. So don't buy any stock before then. But as soon as you can after that, start buying up all the IBM stock you can afford. Daddy was a stockbroker. He left us pretty well-off, though not rich. Mom remembers him shaking his head and saying, 'If only I had been around when IBM was starting off and could have bought some early stock.' Mom still handles our portfolio herself, and she's teaching me."

Allison went on to tell him the names of a few other companies that might help make him rich. It made her kind of nervous and giddy at the same time to be tampering with the future. But she was already changing history, wasn't she?

Despite their talking, they were able to catch a few rosy-blue trout.

"I'll miss eating your special fire-roasted fish," Allison said. "I'll probably never be able to eat fish again without thinking of this place"—she glanced around at the waterfall, the pines, and the dark pool; then her eyes rested on Joshua—"and you."

Joshua put down their fishing poles. He turned her toward him and held both her hands. His eyes were serious as they searched hers.

"I made a commitment to Becky," he began slowly, "and I have to keep my promise and take care of her. I do love her... but I'll never forget you, Allison. What I feel for you, I've never felt before."

Allison noticed that he never admitted he loved her, never actually said the words, but something in the tone of his voice and in the way he looked at her when he spoke told her he did. She suspected such an admission might be too painful. What would be gained by it, anyway? She had less than two days left in his world. But maybe the words didn't need to be said... at least not in this lifetime.

"What will you tell Becky, Joshua?"

"I don't know. She doesn't seem to remember anything about you."

"Of course not. I don't exist yet. At least not for her. She only meets me when she dies. So far, she's still alive. And if we're lucky, she'll stay that way."

Joshua winced at her words. "So what do I say? How do I explain something I can barely believe myself?"

"Maybe it's best if you don't even try. She only needs to know the main facts, not the details. Just tell her what happened while she had blacked out. Tell her about Sadie and José and the Cardona Pomales family and whatever happens to them in the next two days. The only people who need to know I was ever here are you and Magda. It'll be our little secret." Allison watched him sadly. "After a while, it'll be as if I never existed. You'll forget about me."

"I promise you, Allison, and I never break my promises. I will never forget you. Ever."

And with that, he leaned over and placed his lips on hers.

CHAPTER 27

Early the next afternoon, Allison and Joshua snuck along the edge of the woods to the back of the Thompson cabin. The hot day was stifling.

"Should we wait here?" said Allison.

"The window is in the front," Joshua replied.

"Sadie or Don Carlos might catch us if we listen by the window."

"But we can't stay back here. We won't be able to hear anything."

"What if"—Allison swallowed—"what if we were able to hide *inside* the cabin?"

Joshua looked at her as though she'd been speaking a foreign language. "Inside that tiny place?"

"Have you ever been inside Becky's cabin?"

"Well, no. Can't say's I have. But you only have to look at the outside to know there's no place to hide—"

"But there is," Allison said, remembering the small dark cabin. "There's a loft above the bed. And there's a curtain to hide it."

Joshua looked past Allison, his eyes narrowing,

remembering. "Becky's loft. That's where she sleeps. She told me it's the one place she gets any privacy. Sadie is too big to go up there."

"Now, if we can figure out how to get inside unnoticed..." Allison's mind was racing, searching for a plan.

"You're serious! You expect us to get inside the cabin without Sadie noticing and to lie up there in that tiny loft while Sadie and Don Carlos go at it like two angry dogs?"

"They'll be too busy arguing to pay attention to anything else. And we'll be quiet."

Joshua shook his head in disbelief. "Do you know what would happen if they got wind of us spying on them?"

Allison said nothing. She simply stared at him, resolute in her plan.

"They'd rip us to shreds, that's what! Don Carlos is paying Sadie off because he doesn't want *anyone* to know his secret. He may even want to kill her because of it. If he catches us, he may decide to do the same to us."

"We'll just have to be careful," Allison replied. "We have to risk it. It's the only place to hide where we can be sure to hear everything they say."

"Crazy," Joshua muttered, shaking his head. "Just plain crazy."

Ignoring him, Allison placed her ear against the cabin wall. "I think she's in there. Yes, I hear her boots stomping around. Darn! I was hoping—"

The front door creaked open and slammed shut. They heard the *thump, thump, thump* of boots hitting the three front steps.

"Allison, c'mon!" Joshua grabbed her arm and led her away from the cabin, toward the shelter of the trees. "We can't let her spot us."

They reached the trees in time to see Sadie lumbering around the corner of the cabin, carrying a pail and a hoe. Her face was hidden behind the broad brim of a floppy sun hat. At the edge of a small vegetable patch near the far side of the cabin, she set down the pail and hoe and leaned over to inspect a short vine of peas that was beginning to climb a wooden stake.

"She's going to do some weeding," said Joshua. "That used to be Becky's job. Bet she's mad as a tipped cow that she's stuck with doing it herself."

"Serves her right, abusing Becky the way she did."

They watched the large woman inspect a few more plants, then begin the laborious task of hoeing out weed after weed and tossing them into the pail. Every so often, she would straighten up, place her hand on her back, and arch backward, then side to side. Sometimes she would pluck a handkerchief from her pocket and mop the sweat from her face. When the pail was full, she would walk to the edge of the woods, dump the weeds, and slowly hobble back.

"Joshua," Allison said the second time Sadie walked the pail to the edge of the woods, "I have an idea. Let's start creeping back to the cabin. Next time Sadie empties the pail, we'll sneak up to the side of the house and in the front door. She can't hear us when she's at the woods."

"Allison, this is a crazy thing to do, girl."

"Are you with me, or am I going alone?"

Joshua gave a resigned sigh. "I'm with you."

Keeping a wary eye on Sadie Thompson, they scurried along the edge of the forest, scrambling from one tree to the next until they were parallel with the cabin but could still see Sadie's shadow hoeing, bending, tossing, hoeing, bending, tossing. When Sadie stood up, pail in hand, and headed for the woods, the pair tore off across the open patch of land between the woods and the cabin.

When they reached the front door, Joshua crept to the edge of the cabin and peered around the corner. "She's dumping the weeds. Hurry, open the door."

On tiptoes, Allison stole up the three steps and creaked open the door. She hurried inside, and holding the door for Joshua, whispered, "I made it, Joshua. Hurry!"

He rushed up the wooden steps with remarkable stealth and eased the door shut behind him. Allison was already creeping up the rickety ladder to the loft. She flopped onto the straw mattress and scooted across it till she reached the wall. Joshua scooched in next to her, swiftly drawing the curtain back just enough to hide them.

The loft was stuffy and tight. Bits of straw poked through the mattress, scratching Allison's face. She eased herself into a position she could hold for the duration of their vigil. But they didn't have to wait long before the distant sound of hooves pounding dry earth met their ears.

Soon, heavy hurried footsteps approached, climbed the wooden steps, and paused as the door was thrown open. The door slammed shut, and the footsteps—so close Allison had to hold her breath—marched around the cabin. Then they walked briskly to the fireplace, and Allison heard a soft *thud,* a creaking, and a sigh as Sadie sank onto the wooden rocker.

The only sounds in the cabin were the *creak, tap, creak, tap, creak* of Sadie's rocking, the raspy wheeze of

Joshua's stifled breathing, and the *thu-thump, thu-thump* of Allison's heart pounding. In the background, the hoofbeats grew louder.

A few moments later, the hoofbeats stopped, and the door burst open.

"Good afternoon, Don Carlos," said Sadie, still rocking. "Did you bring them?"

Don Carlos stepped to the table and placed something on it with a loud *thump, clang.* "They are here, as I promised," he said in a gruff voice. "Now it is your turn to keep a promise. If that is something of which you are capable."

Sadie gave a low chuckle. "I'll keep my end of the bargain as soon as you keep yours. Where's the horse and wagon?"

"They will be delivered first thing in the morning. Then I want you to clear out and never come back. I will not pay you another penny of blackmail."

Sadie chuckled again.

"I warn you, woman. If you ever come onto my land again, I will shoot you as a trespasser. After tomorrow, this property reverts to me."

Sadie snorted. "The high-and-mighty Don Carlos Cardona Pomales has spoken, is that right? You order it, and it is done. And if anything or anyone dares go against your wishes, you make sure to correct the situation. Pull the right strings, pay the right price, dispose of the right evidence. But it's all catchin' up to you." Sadie gave a bitter laugh. "All your well-planned schemes are startin' to unravel. When your womenfolk find out what you've done—"

"I've done nothing! And you have been well paid to

keep your mouth shut about anything you *think* you know." Don Carlos's tone was menacing. He began taking slow, deliberate steps toward Sadie. "I paid you one hundred dollars in gold coins. Still you wanted more. I've brought you the solid-gold candlesticks you wanted, and you'll have the horse and wagon. But still you want more. Perhaps the only way to silence you is to silence you permanently."

Sadie laughed and continued rocking. *Creak, tap, creak, tap.* "You don't scare me, Don Carlos. You wouldn't dirty your lily-white hands with killing the likes of me. You'd hire someone else to do it. Like you did with José Velásquez."

Allison sucked in her breath.

The sound of Don Carlos's advancing footsteps stopped.

"Oh, you didn't think I knew about that one, did you? Ned confessed everything to me on his deathbed. He said he couldn't take those dreadful secrets to his grave. He hoped telling me would help absolve him. Poor fool! He was a good man but a weak one. And you have a way of usin' people's weaknesses, don't you, Don High-and-Mighty Cardona Pomales?"

"You know nothing of what you speak."

"I know, all right. I know everything you did and more. I know what Ned did. He was fond of José. He needed the money you was offerin', but he couldn't live with the boy's blood on his hands." Sadie stopped rocking. The room was eerily silent except for Don Carlos's heavy intakes of breath. Allison's heart pounded in her ears.

"Would you like to know what he did with the boy, Don High-and-Mighty?"

Don Carlos said nothing.

"Of course, you would. You're dyin' to know. Well, I'm going to tell you, and because I'm not a greedy woman, I won't ask for anything more from you. I just needed something to tide me over in my old age. My eyes are goin', and now you've got my Becky. Isn't it ironic? She can remind you of Ned and me and—"

"Get on with it, woman! What did Ned do with Velásquez?"

"Impatient now, are we? All right, I'll tell you. Ned didn't want to kill the boy, as you'd ordered. But he knew José was headstrong and anything short of death would bring him right back after that girl of yourn. So he arranged for José to be shanghaied. The boy was bound and gagged and sent off on a ship headed for China or Africa or somewheres. Ned got news later that José was shipwrecked and drowned."

Don Carlos let out a deep breath.

"Relieved, are you?" Sadie chuckled. "Well, don't be. He's alive."

"He's what? How do you know this?"

"Because he's here. Paid me a little visit earlier. Looking for Ned, thinking Ned could help him—Ned bein' his pa's old friend and all." She laughed again.

"What—what did you tell him?"

"Told him the truth. No matter what you may think of me, I'm no liar."

"You told him about—"

"No, I didn't spill your precious secret. That's still safe with me...so long as you hold up your end of the bargain."

"Yes, yes, woman. What did you tell him?"

"I just told him that Ned was dead, and that I was his second wife—that he'd married me soon after Ruth died to help him take care of their sweet little Becky." Sadie gave out a loud snort of laughter as if she'd just told a clever joke.

"Stop that cackling, woman, and tell me what he said. Did he ask about Isa?"

"Do pigs eat slop? Course, he asked about her. What the devil do you think he's doing here?"

Allison heard a few quick footsteps move across the floor and a scuffling noise.

"Let go of me!" cried Sadie.

"If you do not tell me what I need to know, woman, I swear to you by the Holy Virgin, I will strangle you right here."

"Don't hurt me!" she shrieked. "I said I'd tell you, and I will. Just let go." The rocker creaked as Sadie sat back down. "That's better. Let me catch my breath."

"Do not lie to me, woman. Speak quickly. How do you know it was José?"

"It wasn't easy—he's changed. Gone through some rough times, that one. And he never told me who he was. But I noticed that crescent-shaped scar on his forehead, and his right arm has the awful burn from when he saved his sister from the fire. I remember from when I used to work at the mansion. He was such a handsome young man, but he only had eyes for Miz Isa." Sadie's voice took on a dreamy tone and drifted off.

"Yes, yes, go on. That sounds like him."

"Like I told you, he asked about Ned. When I told him Ned was dead, he asked if I knew the Cardona Pomales family. Guess he didn't remember me now that I've lost my girlish figure," Sadie said with a bitter laugh. "I told him I used to be their seamstress, and he asked whether I knew anything about Miz Isa. I told him the truth—that she went insane after her lover disappeared and her baby died."

"You told him about the baby?" Don Carlos whispered in a tone of disbelief.

"Only that she believed it died. José got real upset at that and asked me more about the baby and where Isa was now. I told him her loving papa keeps her locked up in the west wing of his estate like some kind of animal."

"You told him that?" Don Carlos yelled the words.

"It's the truth, ain't it? You ain't paying me not to tell anyone Miz Isa is insane. Only to not tell that her baby lived and that her pa made sure his family never knew about it by—"

"Be silent, woman, or I *will* silence you! That is a lie you fabricated or Ned told you while he was delusional. You will never utter a word of it to anyone, do you understand?"

"You're sure paying a lot of money to keep a lie secret."

"That is my business. Are you certain you said nothing of this to Velásquez?"

"He'll find out soon enough on his own. He's not delicate and soft-in-the-head like your Isa, or hiding from the truth like your wife. Mark my words, Señor Hoity-Toity, sooner or later, your dirty little secret will be discovered. Then even God may not forgive you."

CHAPTER 28

"Over here, Allison," Joshua said, leading her along the edge of the forest after they left the cabin. "This is where Sadie disappeared. She was carrying something wrapped in white cloth and looking around as if she thought someone might spot her."

"Probably going off to hide the gold candlesticks. Maybe she hid the gold coins, too. Can you tell where she went?"

"Shhhh," Joshua warned, holding a finger to his lips. He pointed to a barely worn path and gestured for her to follow him. They crept along the path, pausing frequently to listen. Soon they heard the sound of scuffling and dry leaves crunching.

Joshua motioned for Allison to stay while he went ahead. She was about to protest when they heard grunting and another scuffle. Joshua darted ahead and ducked under a bush. Allison hiked up her skirts and followed him.

Together they peered through the branches. At the foot of a huge tree, Sadie was tugging a heavy boulder away from the trunk. On the ground lay a bundle wrapped in a white pillowcase.

She grunted and groaned until she had hauled the boulder far enough from the tree to reveal a large hollow at the bottom of the trunk. Sadie sank onto the boulder and heaved a deep sigh. Then she turned to the tree and pulled a burlap bag from the hollow. The bag appeared heavy, and it clanged as she lifted it and untied the top.

Sadie unwrapped the white pillowcase and drew out two solid-gold candlesticks. As she examined them, the raised, ornate surfaces caught the soft afternoon sunlight and reflected it onto the surrounding brush. She gave a satisfied grunt and tucked them back in the pillowcase, then lay them carefully in the burlap bag.

Before retying the bag, Sadie unbuttoned the top of her blouse and removed something from around her neck.

"This should see me through my old age." She chuckled, holding up a thick golden rope. At the end of the rope, the ruby-studded cross glittered in the afternoon sun.

Allison's eyes opened wide; she squeezed Joshua's arm. In amazed silence they watched Sadie bend and place the cross inside the burlap bag.

"On second thought...," she muttered, retrieving the cross and replacing it around her neck. She tucked it back inside her blouse and shoved the bag inside the tree. "You'll be safe here till morning."

With a satisfied grunt, she heaved herself off the boulder, wiggled it back in front of the hollow, and hobbled down the path toward the cabin. Before Allison and Joshua could move, they heard Sadie gasp.

"What're you doin' here?"

Allison and Joshua froze. Since their view of the newcomer was obstructed by trees and brush, Allison's ears became antennae straining to pick up every sound.

"I said, what're you doin' here? How did you get away?" Sadie's voice became high-pitched and whiny. "Why're you staring at me like that?"

"You are the woman," said a soft female voice. Allison had to strain to hear.

"What woman? I don't know what you're talking about."

"The woman, that night..."

"Go back home. Go on. I don't know what you're—"

"You know, don't you? Tell me where my baby is." The voice had a dreamy childlike quality.

"I don't know what you're talkin' about. Now, let me be—I don't got time for your nonsense. Go on home, now, you hear?"

"I heard you tell Papá my baby is still alive. I always knew it. I heard its cry the night it was born. I hear its cry still. Tell me where my baby is. Please tell me."

"Get out of my way, Miz Isa." The edge of nervousness was gone from Sadie's voice. She was back in control. "Go home and ask your papa. Ask him what he did with your baby. Ask him what he did with José."

"José? My José?"

Sadie snickered. "Well, he never was mine. Only had eyes for you, he did. Lot of good it did him."

"I am going to meet José tonight. He is coming for me. He sent me the ruby cross. It means that if he cannot get to me, I should meet him in our secret place. I'll go to the edge of the world and wait—forever, if I have to. And now I have a surprise for him. I will take him our baby."

"And just how're you goin' to do that, Miz Isa?" Sadie's voice was beginning to take on a sarcastic tone.

"You know where my baby is. You told Papá. I could tell he believed you. He was very angry and frightened. Papá does not readily show fear."

"Maybe you're not as cra—as affected as they think," Sadie said dryly. "But there's nothing more I can tell you, Miz Isa. Your papa don't take kindly to anyone who spoils his plans. I have nothing to tell you. Ask him."

"I cannot ask Papá. You know I cannot," she said, beginning to sound agitated. "If I go back there, he will lock me up. Then I may never find my baby or see José again."

"Well, I'm sorry about that. But if I tell you anything, he'll know it was me. There's no tellin' what he'd do. No, if I were to tell you, I'd have to be assured I could get away from here and have enough to live on…"

"You want me to pay you? I would give you anything—everything I own to get my baby back, but"—Isa stifled a sob—"I have nothing."

Sadie snorted. "You're an heiress!"

"I have nothing! Papá disinherited me when I eloped with José. I cannot risk going back and asking Tere for help. And Mamá has already betrayed me once."

"Well, now, that's just too bad."

"No! Do not go."

Allison heard the sound of a scuffle.

"Git out of my way, Miz Isa, or I'll forget my so-called place."

"You cannot leave without telling me," Isa cried.

"You give me no reason to tell you."

"You are a greedy woman! Papá paid you a great deal of money to keep quiet, I know he did. He promised to pay you, and he always keeps his word."

"The holy word of the Cardona Pomales, eh? And is my word any less honorable? He paid me to keep my mouth shut, and by takin' his money I promised to do just that. But you expect me to break my word just because you're the hoity-toity Isabel Cardona Pomales?"

"You, honorable?" Isa shrieked. "You're a despicable blackmailer with a heart of serpents! *¡Desgraciada!* You know how I am suffering, yet you only wish to profit from my misery."

While Sadie and Isa were arguing, Allison and Joshua crept along the path, hiding behind low bushes, until they had a good view.

"Whoa, calm down now, missy," said Sadie. "I didn't mean to get you—"

"Tell me where my baby is!" Isa screamed. "My child could be in danger, or suffering! I know my baby needs me. Now tell me!"

"Stay where you—"

"Tell me!" With the scream of a mountain lion, Isa lunged forward, tackling Sadie at the waist and throwing her to the ground. "You will tell me where my baby is, or I will strangle it out of you!"

The heavy woman collapsed on her back, the wind knocked out of her, with what might as well have been a crazed lioness ripping and clawing at her chest. Suddenly, Isa froze.

"Abuelita's ruby cross?" Isa held the cross, still attached to the gold rope around Sadie's neck. "What are you doing with this?"

"He—he gave it to me."

"José would never simply give you my cross. *¡Canalla!* What have you done to him? Where is he?"

"Get off—" Sadie began to struggle.

In less than a second, Isa was sitting on Sadie's chest, pinning the woman's struggling arms with her knees. She yanked the golden rope over Sadie's head and slipped it over her own. Then she entwined her strong fingers in the woman's gray-streaked hair. Screaming, Isa lifted Sadie's head by the hair and pounded it into the ground. Over and over, she lifted and pounded, lifted and pounded.

"*¡Canalla!*" she cried. "*¡Desgraciada!* Where is my baby?"

"Joshua," Allison half whispered, half cried, "she'll kill Sadie!"

The next moment, Joshua, with Allison close behind, was sprinting to Sadie's aid. He grabbed Isa from behind, wrapping his arms around hers. But Isa was wild and much too strong. She pushed him backward and ripped herself free. Before he could get up, Isa fled into the forest.

Allison leaped over Joshua and raced after her. She could hear Joshua's footsteps close behind.

"Isa," she called, "come back! Please come back. We want to help you."

But Isa kept running, her wild hair like flames streaming after her, and soon, she vanished into the woods.

When they returned to the spot where they had left Sadie, she, too, had disappeared.

CHAPTER 29

As the shadows of evening crept like a dark specter over the meadow, blending the edges of the cabin with those of nearby trees, Allison and Joshua snuck to the edge of the clearing.

Sadie's silhouette was plainly visible against the soft yellow light of the lantern as she paced back and forth behind the drawn curtains of the tiny kitchen window. Smoke wafted from the stovepipe, bringing with it the aroma of roasting meat and reminding Allison she hadn't eaten since noon.

Joshua's stomach grumbled. "She's there, can we go now? I'm starving."

"I guess we managed to save her from being murdered. She's not likely to go back out tonight or let anyone inside. That should keep her safe. At least, till tomorrow morning."

"Good, so can we go?"

"Hmmm, in a minute," Allison replied absently. "Joshua, how do you suppose Sadie got the ruby cross? José couldn't have given it to her. He didn't have it anymore, and we gave it to Magda."

"Maybe she stole it from Magda. Did you notice some of the stuff she had in that burlap bag?"

"No, I couldn't see the bag very well. Sadie was in the way."

"Well, I could," Joshua said in a disgusted tone. "I saw a silver candelabra and some other silver and gold trinkets Sadie Thompson could never afford. They all came from the estate. Remember what Miz Teresa said about things disappearing when Sadie was around? She stole them, sure's I'm standing here."

"Probably planning for her old age," Allison muttered. Then she shook her head. "I don't get it. How could she have gotten the ruby cross away from Magda?" She paused. "What if—what if you were right about José? What if he did contact Magda before tonight? Like yesterday when you were preoccupied with Becky and I was back in the future?"

"You think José went to see Magda?"

"We haven't seen Magda for two days. For all we know, he may have been hiding out with her all this time. And Magda may have shown him the ruby cross, explaining how she knew he was still alive. He could have taken it back then—it was his."

"Are you thinking Sadie didn't really give away that information about Miz Isa and the baby the way she told Don Carlos?"

"It would make sense. Sadie wouldn't give away that kind of information for free. She might even have told José about Don Carlos wanting him killed and how instead Ned had him shanghaied."

"All in exchange for the ruby cross?" Joshua considered that for a moment. "But it doesn't make sense. If

José talked to Magda, she would have told him the baby wasn't stillborn. He didn't have to pay to learn that."

Allison shook her head. "Joshua, don't you see? Magda only knew the baby was born alive. She didn't know what happened to it afterward. It could have been sick and died soon after. She had no idea Don Carlos had conspired with someone to get rid of the baby. There's more to the secret than what we heard. Remember? Don Carlos never let Sadie finish telling what she knew."

"That's true. We still don't know what happened to the baby. And Sadie refused to tell Isa."

Allison shuddered at the first thought that entered her head. "Oh, Joshua," she said, feeling ill. "What if he did something horrible to it?"

"You mean had the baby...killed? His own grandchild? Like it was a litter of unwanted kittens?"

"How horrid! How could anyone want to harm a baby?"

"All I know is that Don Carlos is a very proud and controlling man. His daughter ran off with someone he didn't approve of, and she was in the family way."

"But she was married."

Joshua glanced at Allison, then looked away. "They weren't married. They never got a chance—Don Carlos stopped the ceremony. The baby was illegitimate. That's why they eloped—Miz Isa was already...with child. When Don Carlos found out, he rushed Miz Isa away to the convent. He didn't want anyone outside the family to know...about the baby."

"But to do something so cruel and heartless to his daughter, whom he claims to love, and to his own grandchild..."

"He couldn't stand the shame she brought to him and to his family name."

"So if he got José and the baby out of the way, he could erase the past and start again with Isa. He'd simply marry her off to some unsuspecting landowner. And no one would ever know. He's crazier than Isa."

"But Isa spoiled his plans by refusing to keep quiet about José and her baby," said Joshua, "and then going crazy." Allison and Joshua grew silent, thinking about the sad fate of Isa and José and their innocent baby.

After a while, Allison said, "Something's still bugging me: If José knows this deep dark secret, why hasn't he confronted Don Carlos with it?"

"You're right," said Joshua. "If I was him, I'd be fit to be tied. Maybe we should go back to Magda's and find out what she knows. José might be there now."

José was not at Magda's when they arrived. He was out looking for Isa.

Magda ladled out hearty bowls of stew and set them before Allison and Joshua. Between bites they caught each other up on what had happened in the past two days.

"*Pobre* Isa," said Magda, taking a seat at her rocker when everyone had finished eating. "Don Carlos is frantic, acting as though it is her welfare rather than his own that concerns him. When he reached home this afternoon—after his visit with Sadie, from what you tell me—he learned that Isa had escaped, leaving Socorro drugged and bound. Tere was trying to calm her mother and remained with her while Don Carlos and some of his men have begun to scour the forest.

"He came here, certain to find Isa and José, but found

only me. He issued threats and mandates and swore he would finish my brother if he ever again went near Isa. Then he stormed away."

"Where was José?" asked Allison.

"He has been in and out for the past two days, trying to figure out how to break into the mansion and get to Isa. He was dressed in that horrible disguise so no one from the estate would recognize him." Magda shuddered. "I barely recognized him myself when I first saw him. I told him Isa would be terrified if she saw him like that—her mind is so fragile, who knows what she might think. He finally agreed and changed back into his own clothes.

"When José came back this afternoon, he was all excited about something Sadie had told him. He was about to tell me, but first, he wanted to know why Don Carlos was here. He had seen his white horse and stayed hidden until Don Carlos left. After I told him that Isa had escaped and that Don Carlos was searching for her, José became frantic and ran out. I called to him, begging him to wait, telling him that Isa sometimes comes here when she gets out. But he said he couldn't take the chance that Don Carlos or his men might find Isa first."

"I hope he finds her before morning," said Allison. "Tomorrow is April eighteenth, the day of the most devastating earthquake in the history of the United States. She shouldn't be out in the forest alone."

Allison and Joshua decided the safest thing to do was to spend the night with Magda. That way, neither of them would be near the cliff the morning of the earthquake.

As she had before, Allison curled up in Magda's extra

comforter next to the fireplace. At the other side of the fireplace, Joshua set out his bedroll.

Allison's sleep was fitful. She kept having flashback dreams of running through the forest in the dark, of being chased and tripping over Sadie's dead body, of blood smeared and sticky on her hands and feet, of being hurled over the side of the cliff and plummeting down, down, down…

She awoke with a start, her heart beating to the rhythm of hoofbeats in the distance, closer, closer, then fading away. She glanced around. The fire had begun to burn down, but enough light remained to see shapes in the room. She glanced at Joshua's bedroll.

It was empty.

Her heart leaped into her throat, settling back only to begin a thunderous pounding that filled her ears like the rhythmic roar of a waterfall. The fire of panic shot through her limbs. Where was he? What could possibly have made him leave the cottage?

Allison tore away her covers and tiptoed to Magda's curtain. She peeked inside. Magda was sound asleep, her breathing soft and rhythmic.

Her heart still pounding in her ears, Allison cracked open the front door and peered outside. The night was dark: Only pale moonlight etched the shape of trees beyond the cottage. Nothing moved, nothing made a sound, nothing but Allison appeared alive.

"Find him," a voice whispered in her ear. "Find Joshua."

Allison wondered whether she had heard a voice at all. Perhaps it was her thoughts, loud enough in the stillness of the night to be heard in her ears rather than in her head. That was after all the strongest impulse she was feeling: the desire to find Joshua. It pulsed through the blood that her heart was pumping so strongly in her veins and through the nerves that were creaking inside her limbs like Magda's old rocker. It was only natural that the impulse be translated into a thought so strong it would sound like a voice in her ears.

She stepped into the yard to have a better look around. Still nothing moved.

"Where could he be?" she muttered under her breath. "Joshua, you fool, how could you go off on your own, tonight of all nights?"

It occurred to her that he might have decided to visit the waterfall cave. Maybe he couldn't sleep. She could go as far as the cave and check it out. It couldn't hurt just to go that far. She'd feel better knowing where he was.

When she arrived at the site of the crashing waters, she shivered at the similarity between this night and the other time she had lived through the night of April 17, 1906. Even the moon was identical: a silver sliver hanging among a sprinkling of stars. But of course it was identical—it had to be. In the continuum of time and space, this was the very same night.

That Joshua! If he hadn't wandered off, she wouldn't be reliving any of this. In a huff, she picked up her skirts and hurried along the rocky path behind the waterfall to the tiny cave. As with the other time, the cave was deserted, and the bed appeared untouched.

"Oh, Joshua, where could you be?" she wailed aloud. "Well, that does it. I'm going back to Magda's. If he's not there by now, maybe Magda will know where he is."

Allison returned to the forest path and began to wind

her way back to the cottage. Halfway there she heard a twig crack and leaves crumble. Her heart jumped. She stood still, listening.

Another twig cracked. Then another.

Her first instinct was to hide behind a bush. It could be just a night prowler—a possum, a raccoon, even Bubba. But at that instant, a voice in her head screamed: "Run! Save me!"

Before she could think, her legs came alive. As if she were a mechanical toy manipulated by remote control, she found herself running deeper and deeper into the forest. All she could do was hold her arms in front of her face to protect it from the ripping claws of outstretched branches.

All the while, the voice screamed: "Hurry, hurry! He's coming. *Run!*"

The panic that raced through her veins, and the voice that screamed in her ears and filled her brain, kept her mind a jumble. Somewhere inside her, Allison knew she was doing the wrong thing. She shouldn't run—she should think. But she couldn't make her brain listen, and she couldn't stop Becky's body from panicking. She felt as though she were reliving her last conscious moments, just after the red Mercedes sent her flying over the ravine. She was locked in a body she couldn't control, seeing herself flying down, down, down when things had turned around and the rocks below her began to rush up, up, up.

"No!" she screamed. "Nooooo! Sto-oop!"

But Becky's body continued to run, shrieking back, "Save me! Save me!"

Listen to me, Becky, she spoke to the girl in her head. *Stop screaming and listen to me!*

"Help me! Run!" Becky screamed.

SHUT UP, BECKY!

The screaming stopped, but Becky's body kept running.

Listen to me. I am trying to save you, but you've got to let me. Now, slow down.

Allison could feel her legs begin to slow.

"Please don't let me die," Becky whimpered.

Becky, you've got to trust me. Let me think. Let me get us through this. Go back to the hospital. I need you there, Becky. And you need me here. Go back, and let me think.

With a tiny whimper, Becky released control of her body. Becky seemed to be gaining strength in the past—she must be, to have been able to take control of her body like that. Did that also mean she was weakening in the future? Would she be strong enough to keep Allison's body alive through surgery? Allison realized she needed to resolve Becky's problem in the past and get back to her own body as soon as possible.

She slowed to a trot, then stopped completely, listening to the sounds of the forest. Her breath was coming in such loud, rough pants she could barely hear the *thump-thump* of heavy footsteps in the distance. Someone was coming closer, either on his own or following her.

She decided to stay out of sight but not to panic. For all she knew, it might be Joshua. But it also might be Sadie, or someone equally dangerous. She needed to find a good place to hide. Tucking her head to avoid branches, she continued to run down the path, but this time, listening and looking.

Within a few minutes, she broke through the trees into a clearing. It looked familiar. It seemed to be the same clearing she had encountered when she noticed the blood on her hands and dress.

Resisting the panic that bubbled inside her stomach, she held out her hands, allowing the moonlight to illuminate them. They appeared clean. She let out a deep breath. Of course, they were. She hadn't tripped over a dead body and slipped in its blood. Not this time. She looked down. Her dress was the emerald-green gown, not the faded calico. And it was still clean.

Time was not repeating itself. She had broken the chain.

An explosion of twigs cracking and branches being bent to breaking and snapping back reminded Allison she still had a job to do. She ducked beneath a thick cluster of bushes, peering out in time to see a figure crash through the branches and halt a few feet away, stooping forward and wheezing.

It was all happening again. Maybe she hadn't broken the chain after all.

In the dim moonlight, she saw the figure of a man whose head oscillated back and forth, scanning the clearing. But this man was not barefoot and shabbily clad. Nor was his head covered with a grubby black mane of hair. This man looked like he had stepped from the cover of a modern romance novel: long black hair, clean and gleaming like raven feathers in the moonlight and tied at the nape of his neck. His face was strong, handsome, and clean shaven. He wore a white shirt with long, billowy sleeves, black vest and pants, and tall black boots.

The man placed his hands on his knees, apparently trying to catch his breath. His wheezing continued, grating like fingernails over sandpaper.

Allison stretched her neck, trying to get a better look. If only she could find a sign that it was José—maybe the crescent-shaped scar on his forehead or the burn on his right arm. But his arms were covered by the long sleeves, and she could only see the side of his face.

As she rose onto her knees to get a better look, she stepped on a twig.

The man's head snapped toward her, and their eyes met. A look of recognition, then one of disbelief crossed his face. "Isa?" he whispered.

Allison opened her mouth to speak, but nothing would come out. She shook her head.

The man rose to his full height. "Rebecca?" He spoke the name in a strong Spanish accent.

Allison could only stare.

He held out his hand. "Come. Do not be afraid. I will not harm you."

Allison stood but couldn't seem to move her legs. The man stepped toward her, reached out, and took her hand. "Please, come. I promise, I will not harm you."

Despite its strong muscles and tendons, his hand held hers as delicately as if he were holding a thin eggshell. In the light of the moon, she could see the faint shape of a crescent in the middle of his forehead.

"José?" she was finally able to whisper.

A slow smile began to pull the edges of his mouth. But his eyes remained solemn and his gaze fixed on her face. He gave a slight bow from the waist.

"How—how do you know me?" Allison whispered.

José's eyes, glistening like polished onyx, at last softened. "I'd know Isa's child anywhere."

CHAPTER 30

"Allison, where have you been?" Magda was awake and making breakfast—although the sky was still dark, it was already early morning. The look on her face when Allison and José entered the cottage was one of great relief. "Joshua has been frantic."

Allison rushed to Magda's side. "Joshua came back?"

"He couldn't sleep and went out for a walk. When he returned, you were gone. He went back to search the forest for you. I told him José would be looking for you, too, but he insisted on going himself."

"And I must return to search for Isa," José said, pacing the small room. "I must find her before that father of hers—"

"But first you must eat something," Magda insisted. "You need your strength. You do not know when you will be able to eat again."

"Perhaps you are right," he said, finally taking a seat at the table.

Allison, still in awe of Magda's handsome brother *(Becky's father!)*, sat across from him and tried to digest all that had happened since José had found her. She could kick herself for not having guessed earlier. Of course, Becky was Isa's daughter. All the clues had been there, if she'd only paid attention. Doña Ana, when she first saw her, had believed her to be Isa. She and Tere had dismissed the mistake, blaming it on the woman's drugged and confused state. Then there was the way Don Carlos acted around her—hostile and almost frightened. He must have begun to suspect who she was and feared his secret would somehow be revealed. No wonder he didn't want her caring for Isa. If Don Carlos had begun to suspect who Becky was, eventually, Isa might, too. And that was why Becky's face had looked so familiar to her: Becky resembled the seventeen-year-old Isa in the painting.

On the way to the cottage, José told Allison how he had discovered Don Carlos's secret: For the first day and a half of his arrival with Don Carlos's buggy, he hid out in the forest, keeping an eye on the estate while he waited for Isa to get his message—the ruby cross—and trying to figure out his next move. He didn't want to contact Magda right away for fear she would worry and try to talk him out of doing anything dangerous. But on the second night of his return, with no sign of his beloved Isa, he realized he needed to confide in Magda and to find out whether she knew of Isa's whereabouts.

When he finally decided to approach his sister, Magda had company—Becky and Joshua, who he later found out were bringing her the ruby cross. He waited until Becky and Joshua were gone, and was sure Magda was alone, before approaching her. That night, Magda told him all that had happened since he had been shanghaied, and brought him up to date on what had happened since Tere had returned from San Francisco with the cross. When Magda explained that Sadie was blackmailing Don Carlos, José had felt in his gut it had to do with him and Isa. He asked Magda for the ruby cross and gave it to Sadie in exchange for her knowledge. Sadie was more than willing to betray Don Carlos. She told José that Don Carlos had paid Ned Thompson to kill him and to get rid of the baby. But Ned was no murderer. Instead, he devised a plan to take care of both matters without bloodshed. José was shanghaied, and the baby became a blessing.

His wife, Ruth, had given birth to a baby girl, Rachel, only one week before Becky was born. Rachel died two days later, and Ruth was devastated. When offered the opportunity, Ned brought her a new baby—one who needed love and nurturing and a home. Ruth raised the baby until Ruth died of consumption. Soon after that, Ned married Sadie. Two years later, Ned died during an influenza epidemic, but before he died, he confessed his secret to Sadie. Though Sadie wouldn't admit it, José remembered her jealousy of Isa. She hated the Cardona Pomales family and saw a way to make Don Carlos pay. She could get rich at the same time.

That night, while Allison was out looking for Joshua, José had returned to Magda's. It was then that he confessed to Magda about his visit to Sadie's and what he'd found out about his daughter. Magda then told him what Allison had said about Isa's fight with Sadie and asked him to keep an eye out for Becky while he was looking for Isa. He had been as eager to find his daughter as he was to find his beloved.

When Allison looked up from her thoughts, she found José's gaze fixed on her. She felt her cheeks flush.

He smiled. "Forgive me for staring, but you look so much like your mother... when I last saw her. And, after all, it is not every day one meets a fourteen-year-old daughter one did not know one had."

"I just wish I had guessed earlier," Allison replied. She meant that she, Allison, should have guessed. But José misunderstood.

"It was probably just as well you did not," he said. "How could you have confronted Don Carlos on your own?"

"Maybe Tere could have helped." Allison realized the moment she mentioned Tere that she was her aunt, or rather, Becky's aunt.

"Ah, Tere. She certainly has grown, hasn't she?" he said, glancing at Magda. "She was only a child when I last saw her. Fortunately, as it turned out, because she wasn't able to recognize me."

"She has grown into a strong-spirited young woman and a good friend," Magda said.

"I am glad you were well taken care of while I was gone." Then José turned his attention back to Allison. "While I finish eating, perhaps Rebecca can tell me more about Isa's encounter with Sadie Thompson."

Allison told José about her afternoon with Joshua as they spied on Sadie, trying to find out why Sadie was blackmailing Don Carlos. She ended by telling him how she had tried to stop Isa, but Isa had disappeared into the forest.

"It was fortunate you prevented Isa from killing Sadie," said Magda. "Imagine what your lives would be like if she had been a murderess..."

"Very fortunate," José said somberly. Turning to

Allison, he asked, "While Isa spoke to Sadie, did she give any indication of where she might go next?"

Allison felt embarrassed at what she had to confess. "Isa... Isa hasn't been well. She's been obsessed with finding her baby—me, I guess—and about meeting you. We all thought... I mean, no one knew... we thought it was all in her head..."

José nodded sadly. "But now that you know, can you make any sense of what she said?"

"She just said she was going to meet you—" Allison gasped, remembering. "She was going to wait for you at your secret place. She said she'd go to the ends of the earth and wait for you."

José's eyes opened wide. He leaned forward and grabbed Allison's hand, squeezing it none too gently. "Think carefully, child. Did she say she was going to 'the edge of the world'?"

"Well... yes, but I thought it was a mixed metaphor"—the look of confusion in José's eyes made her restate her sentence—"I mean I thought she got the phrase wrong. In English there's an expression: going to the ends of the earth. It means—"

"*Sí, sí,* I know what it means," he said, waving away her words. "I do not know how I could have forgotten. The edge of the world was our secret meeting place: *al borde del mundo*. She named it that because when you stand at the edge of the cliff, it feels as if you are standing at the edge of the world. That must be where she is. I must go to her."

At the mention of the word *cliff,* Allison's heart seemed to stop. The blood rushed from her face. "Cliff? What cliff? Magda, could it be—"

In a rush of Spanish, Magda asked her brother about the cliff. Then she turned to Allison. "It is the same cliff—the one you call Devil's Drop."

Allison felt the room spin. She leaned into the table, gripping the edge until her knuckles turned white.

"Rebecca?" said José. "What is wrong? Magda, help her. The child looks ill."

"No," said Allison, sitting back, "I'll be all right. But you must hurry. The earthquake... the cliff... Isa... you must get to her before dawn."

"What is she talking about, Magda? What earthquake?"

"José, Becky has a premonition—a very strong one—that there will be an earthquake this morning, and that anyone near the cliff... will be killed."

José threw back his chair and in two steps was at the door. He turned to Magda. "I must go. Take care of my daughter."

"No, wait!" cried Allison. "I have to go with you. I have a terrible feeling that that's where Joshua is, too. Looking for me."

CHAPTER 31

The sky was still dark when they arrived at the edge of the forest, above the road that snaked along the ravine. Allison was hot and sweaty and wished she could rip off the heavy skirts that weighed her down. José was wheezing badly.

He led her along a winding path down the side of the hill and to the cliff road. They had to walk about a half mile up the mountain to reach the V of Devil's Drop. As they drew near, they heard yelling around the other side of the V but could not make out the words.

José began to run. Allison followed. When they turned the corner, Allison gasped.

Beside a tall rock formation at the edge of the cliff, almost blocked from view of the road, stood Isa. Her pale blue dress flapped about her legs and her long hair waved behind her as she leaned into the wind toward the ravine below. At that angle, standing so stiff and still, her arms at her side and her face straight ahead, she looked like a ship's figurehead leaning into oncoming waves. The ruby cross dangled from her neck, gleaming in the moonlight.

A few yards away, pleading and crying out to her, stood Don Carlos.

"Madre de Dios," whispered José. He dropped the coil of rope that Allison had insisted they bring and stood as stiff and still as Isa, a look of terror on his face.

"Isa, *mija,* I beg of you, do not do this," cried Don Carlos. The wind was so strong it tossed back his words and sent them hurling toward José and Allison. "Think of your mother, Isa. Think of what this will do to her."

At that, Isa yelled back, "Mamá betrayed me. Mamá does not deserve my love."

"No, Isa, your *mamá* did not betray you. It was me. Punish me, if you like. But not your mother." He paused, struggling for more words. "Think... think of Tere, how she loves you."

"Tere shall be better off without me. I will never go back with you, Papá. Never! I'd rather be dead than locked away in that room for the rest of my life. You took away my José and took away my baby. But you will not have my freedom." Isa raised her arms.

"No!" screamed José and Allison together. They ran to join Don Carlos, afraid to go closer for fear of startling Isa and causing her to fall.

Don Carlos spun around. He looked at José, then at Allison. In quick succession, his expression was transformed from one of horror, as if he'd seen a ghost, to one of supreme relief. He fell to his knees, covering his face with his hands to hide his weeping. "Help her. Help my daughter."

"Get up, old man." José spit out the words. "Tell her I am here. I don't want to make things worse by shocking her."

Don Carlos stared at him, confused. José grabbed the man by the arm and yanked him up. "Tell her!"

"Isa!" Don Carlos cried. "Wait, José is here. And so is"—Don Carlos glanced at Allison—"your daughter."

"*¡Embustero!*" she screamed. "You are nothing but a liar! You are trying to trick me, but it won't work. I'll never go back with you!" She pulled back her arms.

"Rubia! *Mi amor,* it is me—José. I sent you the ruby cross. I told you I was coming. Now I am here." José stepped forward so she could see him.

At the sound of his voice, Isa lowered her arms. Slowly, as if afraid of what she might see, Isa turned.

José held out his arms. For a moment, she looked as if she might faint. She closed her eyes and tilted back her head. Then she looked back at him, lifted her arms, and rushed forward. In her haste, she stepped on a stray rock that lay on the narrow, two-foot-wide ledge, and her foot twisted sideways. She lurched to the side, into the rocky wall, and slid to the ground, landing halfway off the ledge. Her legs dangled in midair.

As José and Don Carlos leaped to her aid, Allison reached out and grabbed Don Carlos's arm. "The ledge is too narrow for the two of you. Let José—let my father help her."

Don Carlos ripped his arm from her grasp. "She is my daughter. It is I who should rescue her."

Allison's eyes blazed. "Haven't you done enough already... Grandfather?" With those words she turned her attention to Becky's parents.

José was kneeling beside Isa, clutching her dress by the waist. He hoisted her up and wrapped his arms around her, burying his face in her golden-red curls. Isa clung to him, sobbing and laughing. After a few minutes, José helped Isa up and walked her carefully away from the ledge, bringing her face-to-face with Allison.

"Ven, mi amor," he said, one arm still wrapped around her waist, "I want you to meet our daughter, Rebecca."

Isa's eyes, already red from crying, spilled more tears. She brought a trembling hand to Allison's face and whispered, "It was you all along. You are my baby."

With the succession of dramatic events, Allison had completely forgotten the time. When she remembered, she gasped. "José, the earthquake! And Joshua. We still haven't found Joshua."

"What is she talking about, Velásquez?" asked Don Carlos, who until then had been standing off to the side. "What earthquake?"

"Rebecca had a *presentimiento*... about a great earthquake—this morning."

Don Carlos rolled his eyes. "You Velásquezes are all the same. Already, this young one is thinking of premonitions."

Allison felt her face burn. "I know what I'm talking about! There will be an earthquake—soon. Just after daybreak. José—Papá—please believe me. We have to find Joshua and get out of here—to lower land. A meadow or something."

José's eyes held the intensity of the night before. He placed his hand on her cheek. "I believe you. Where do you think Joshua is?"

"I—I thought he might have come here, looking for

me. I... told him I'd had a vision of me being here at this cliff during the earthquake... and falling..."

José glanced around. "But you can see he is not here. We have been here at least half an hour—"

"Maybe he's hurt," said Allison, silently praying she was wrong. "Maybe he can't get to us."

José placed his hands on her shoulders. "What do you want us to do?"

Allison struggled for an answer. Finally, she lowered her head in resignation. She couldn't risk endangering all of them.

"We have to go," she said. "We can't stay here much longer. Maybe we can search along the way."

José picked up the coil of rope, and they began their descent along the mountain road. Allison led the way. Don Carlos took the rear, struggling to calm his white horse.

"He has been unusually skittish all morning," Don Carlos explained. "I do not understand it. He is usually a well-behaved animal."

"Animals can sense things," Allison replied. "He knows an earthquake's coming."

Don Carlos snorted and shook his head. Allison ignored him.

Dawn was beginning to brighten the dark sky. As they passed the V of Devil's Drop, Allison noticed a piece of wood lying beside the edge of the cliff. It looked like the branch she had been reaching for when she slid down the cliff to the ledge. The hair on her arms rose.

"Wait," she said, cautiously approaching the edge. As she drew near, she noticed freshly exposed earth, as though the ground had recently been disturbed. She lay on her stomach and slithered to the edge.

"Oh, god," she whispered when she peered over the side. A few yards below, on the same ledge where she had lain, lay Joshua. His eyes were closed.

After all this, she hadn't really broken the chain. They had only reversed roles.

"Joshua?" she called into the strong wind. "Can you hear me?"

Joshua opened his eyes. At first he seemed relieved to see her, then a look of fear crossed his face. "Go back, Allison. Get away before it happens. You have to save Becky."

"No, I won't leave without you. How...how did you fall?"

"I was looking for you. When I couldn't find you, I thought you might have fallen, so I stepped to the edge, and..."

He didn't have to finish. She knew what must have happened. Didn't the same thing happen to her the first time she was here? And to Becky?

Behind her, Allison heard footsteps. She turned her head. "Don't come any closer," she told José. "It's dangerous here. The ground is soft."

José lay down and crawled to her side.

"He's down there," she said. "Joshua."

"Are you hurt, *mijo*?" he called down to Joshua.

Joshua shook his head. The slight movement sent a rush of gravel flying down the cliff. "A little scraped. Other than that, I'm all right. But I can't move because the ledge is too small."

Allison sighed with relief.

"That's good, Joshua," said José. "I'm coming down."

"No!" cried Isa. "I won't lose you again." If Don Carlos had not been holding her, she would have run to José. "Rebecca, come back, you'll be hurt."

Allison turned to Isa. "Isa, Mamá, Joshua is to me what José is to you. We must save him. He wouldn't be in this danger if he hadn't been trying to help me."

Isa stopped struggling. She lowered her head. "Help him, José."

José sat back on his heels and began to tie the rope around his waist. "Did you have a premonition about this rope, too?" he asked Allison.

"Aren't you glad I did?"

"Don Carlos," said José, "can I trust you to hold the rope for me?"

Don Carlos looked surprised. Then his face relaxed. "Velásquez, wait," he said, stepping forward. "Let me go down for the boy. You hold the rope."

"I am ready. There is no need—"

Don Carlos held out his hands, palms up, fingers spread. His arrogance was gone, he looked defeated. "*Por favor,* let me do this one thing. For you... for my granddaughter... for my family..."

José hesitated only a moment. He slipped off the rope and handed it to Don Carlos. The older man tied it around his waist, and the two men crawled to the edge of the cliff.

With José holding the rope, Don Carlos scooted off the edge. Before he slipped from view, he stopped, looked at Allison, and said, "You are a remarkable young woman."

Then he made his way down the cliff, clutching the rope and bouncing off the sides, sending dirt and rocks cascading into the gulch below. When Don Carlos reached Joshua, he perched on the ledge and pulled the boy up. Joshua clung to him awkwardly.

"Have Joshua climb on your back," José called down. "We'll have to bring you both up at the same time. Isa, Rebecca, I need your help."

"What about the horse?" asked Isa.

"We can't risk it," said José. "He's too skittish. There isn't enough rope, anyway."

So Isa grabbed José around the waist while Allison held on to the rope and helped him pull. Together, they hauled the man and the boy up the cliff and over the side to safety.

Allison grabbed Joshua and hugged him as hard as she could. Isa hugged her father.

Dogs howled in the distance. The white horse neighed and stomped the ground.

"The earthquake!" Allison cried. "We have to get out of here!"

"The meadow at the foot of the mountain," said Joshua. "That's the safest place. José, take Miz Isa, but stay on the main road. I'll follow with Al—Becky and Don Carlos. Hurry!"

José grabbed Isa's hand and they began running down the road. Don Carlos took the horse's reins, but as Joshua turned to take Allison's hand, the horse began to dance sideways.

"Whoa, boy!" Don Carlos gripped the reins and tried to stroke the horse's forehead. "Calm down, Nieve. It's all right."

But the horse continued to prance on his front legs. His nostrils flared, exposing hot-pink flesh. His eyes rolled wildly. He tugged back his head, tossing it, trying to shake loose from the reins. At last, he reared up, towering above Don Carlos.

"Get down, Nieve. Down, boy!"

The horse pulled sideways, toward Allison. She jumped back, trying to get out of the way.

Don Carlos turned to Allison. "Look out!" he cried, as Nieve's reins ripped from his hands.

Time switched to slow motion. Allison saw the horse bolt and gallop down the road. Don Carlos, mouth open, a look of terror on his face, struggled toward her as though he were moving through water. Joshua turned from the horse to Don Carlos to Allison. When he saw her, the same expression of terror gripped him. At the same moment, Allison felt the ground slip from under her feet and her body tip backward.

She opened her mouth to scream, but other screams were already filling her brain. "*Save me!*" they cried.

In the next instant, Don Carlos had her by the waist and, in one motion, tossed her into the air toward Joshua. Becky's body kept going, but Allison felt herself lift up into the air and begin to float high above the scene.

She saw Joshua grab Becky as she was propelled through the air, pull her toward him, and fall backward onto the ground, still hugging her tightly. She saw Don Carlos, after catching Becky and throwing her to Joshua, continue to fly forward and over the side of Devil's Drop, into the ravine below. She saw Joshua pull Becky to her feet and run with her down the road. And at the bottom of the hill, she saw Nieve, Don Carlos's white horse, catch up to Isa and José and leave them far behind.

Then she felt a wind wrench her with the force of a

cyclone. But she fought it, not wanting to leave the past until she was sure her friends were safe. She held on until she saw Isa and José reach level ground. José left Isa and ran back to help Joshua with Becky. As the three of them reached Isa's side, the world began to shudder and thunder and roar. The two couples fell to the ground and clung to one another. In the distance, the dirt road undulated like waves on a beach. Trees thrashed left and right and hillsides spewed forth dirt and rocks, then dissolved like heaps of chocolate powder in milk.

The next thing Allison saw was the tunnel as she whirled toward the white light.

PART FIVE

The Letter

Past life and death, I shall transcend
to search for you till heaven's end:
At first, he's someone I don't know—
Until, within his eyes . . . that glow . . .
I recognize—He's you!

CHAPTER 32

I'm floating above a room I don't recognize. It's filled with medical equipment and lights and people wearing pale green scrubs, surgical caps, goggles, and masks. The people huddle over a narrow table on which a body lies covered with a green sheet. Only the head is exposed. It's my head.

It's me lying on that table.

A slow *beep... beep... beep...* dominates the room.

"Something's wrong, doctor," says a nurse.

The slow beeping becomes a long, continuous *beeeeeeeeeppp....*

"Doctor, we're losing her!" someone cries. "Her heart is fibrillating!"

"Bring the crash cart! We're not going to lose her," a woman snaps. "Come on, Allison, fight! Help me out, here. Fight!"

What's wrong? What are they talking about? Am I dying?

I try to sink into my body, but a force like a strong

current pushes me away. Something is pulling me back, back into the wind tunnel.

Becky? Is that you?

Silence.

I try again. The sound of the wind in the distance is growing closer.

Oh, god, no. I must have stayed too long. I waited too long to come back.

I feel the strong tug of the wind tunnel drawing me back, away from the operating room, away from my body. The scene below becomes fuzzy, as if I'm watching it through a gauze filter. The sounds and the voices have become garbled, almost incomprehensible. I'm fighting the backward pull, straining to make out what's happening below.

A nurse rolls a cart to the table and hands the doctor two paddles. The doctor lowers the sheet, places the paddles on either side of my chest, and yells, "Charge to 200 joules! Clear! Shock!"

My body jumps, then lies still.

The doctor glances at a monitor. It shows an erratic squiggle that darts and wiggles across the screen. The eerie *beeeeeeeeeppp* continues.

Someone places a hand on the doctor's shoulder. "Doctor, I don't think—"

The doctor jerks her shoulder, shirking off the hand. She begins to massage my heart, speaking softly. I can barely make out the words: "Allison . . . can do it . . . Come back, Allison."

The doctor again takes the paddles and holds them to my sides. "Charge to 300 joules! Stand clear! Shock!"

My body jumps, bouncing like a solid rubber doll as it lands.

The scene is becoming fuzzier; the voices more distant.

"Dr. Winthrop . . . too late."

Dr. Winthrop? Joshua? Where is he? He can't still be alive, practicing medicine, can he?

The doctor starts pushing her hands into my chest again. ". . . Won't let you die . . . hear me? Fight!"

The doctor stares at the monitor, the monitor with the wriggling line, the monitor that seems to emit the eerie *beeeeep.*

All eyes are on the monitor.

The room is silent except for the sound of the wind and the *beeeeep.*

"Try, Allison . . . ," says the doctor, still massaging my chest, "can't give up . . . time to come back."

I'm fighting, Joshua. Wait for me. I'm trying!

Another jolt of electricity from the paddles, and—

Through the haze, a distinct blip emerges from the haphazard, squiggly pattern on the monitor. It's accompanied by a quick *beep.* The people in the room seem to be holding their breaths. Another blip appears on the now smooth line, then another and another, each accompanied by a tiny *beep,* until they become a constant, rhythmic *beep, beep, beep.*

As if someone turned off a switch, the wind tunnel disappears. A new force draws me down toward the operating table, and with a snap, I'm in my body.

A cheer goes up in the operating room.

I feel a hand on my shoulder and a whisper in my ear: "Welcome back, Allison. Welcome back home."

When I open my eyes, my favorite song is playing. PoPo is lying in the crook of my left arm. Mom's head is resting on my chest. She's snoring softly.

I grin. Slowly, I pull my right arm from under the sheet and stroke Mom's baby-fine hair. A whiff of tea-rose perfume wafts toward me. I inhale.

"Mom?" I whisper.

"Mmmmm?" Mom mumbles.

"Mom, I'm back."

With a start, Mom's head snaps up. She stares at my smiling face.

"I'm back, Mom."

Mom's mouth opens to speak, but instead, she bites her lower lip, brings a trembling hand to my face, and touches my cheek. Tears spill from her eyes.

I remember another scene, so similar, yet so long ago: another mother greeting a child she thought she might never see again. My eyes grow heavy. I suddenly feel so tired. I close my eyes and sleep.

CHAPTER 33

As I gather my things and place them in the box Mom brought, preparing for my long-awaited release from the hospital, someone steps up behind me.

"Allison?" says a familiar male voice. A voice that I thought I'd never hear again. A voice that has haunted my dreams since I awoke from the coma two weeks ago.

"Joshua?" I can barely whisper the name.

"Are you Allison Blair?" the voice repeats.

"Joshua, it *is* you!" I spin around only to come face-to-face with a stranger. A boy, about my age, smiles apologetically. His onyx-black eyes twinkle with the humor of an untold joke. His elfin smile is infectious.

"No, I'm Jonah—Jonah Sloane. My mother is your neurosurgeon. But my great-grandfather's name was Joshua."

I must be dreaming! I place my hand on the bed to stop my legs from collapsing beneath me. My heart beats as quickly as if I'd been running a marathon.

"Are you all right?" Jonah reaches out to keep me

from falling. "Maybe you'd better sit down." He helps me onto the bed.

His touch is so familiar...so right. I lick my lips. My mouth is suddenly dry. "Your g-grandfather was Joshua? W-Winthrop?"

"Mmm-hmm, yes—great-grandfather," Jonah replies, pulling up a chair next to my bed and making himself comfortable. "You must be wondering why I'm here."

I can only nod, and stiffly at that.

"My mom—Dr. Winthrop-Sloane? Well, like I told you, she's your surgeon. She was called away—out of state. Mom wanted to give you this herself"—Jonah holds out a sealed, ivory-colored envelope—"but she won't be back for at least a week. Apparently, this thing's been in a safe for a while, and Mom had her lawyer bring it to me. She wanted you to have it on the day you left the hospital."

Jonah grins—it's Joshua's grin. My heart jumps.

"I guess I get to be the emissary," he says.

With a shaking hand, I reach for the envelope. My full name, *Allison Anne Blair,* is written in bold black script on the front. The envelope looks yellow with age. I turn it over. A large blue wax seal with the initials JW is burned in the center.

My fingers tremble as I break the seal. The letter is written in the same bold script that appears on the envelope. I wipe the sweat from my hands and try to keep them from shaking as I read the words.

Jonah rises. "Well, I guess I'd better leave you alone... to read the letter."

"No!" I cry. Then embarrassed at my outburst, I add, "I mean, please...stay. I don't think I can read this alone."

Jonah flashes me another heart-stopping smile and sits back down. "Never could resist a damsel in distress."

April 18, 1956

My Dearest Allison:

Today is the fiftieth anniversary of the Great Earthquake, and I feel it is fitting to commemorate the date by writing you the letter I've been waiting years to write.

I told you I would never forget you. I hope this proves I never did. And if this letter finds you, I hope it is because in some small way, I was able to give back to you what you gave to Becky and me—life.

I am embarrassed to confess that until I fell onto the ledge that morning fifty years ago, I did not truly believe you could be from the future. I wanted to believe, and I trusted you with all my heart and soul. But it was blind trust, based on what I felt for you. The occurrence of the earthquake and the terrible fires and damage in San Francisco provided further proof of your existence. The fact you never returned after Becky was saved was the final proof. I miss you more than I can express.

I wish I could tell you our story had a fairy-tale ending and we all lived happily ever after. Some parts were good, very good. But as Magda always said, you have to take the good with the bad.

Fate wanted two lives from our small group on April 18, 1906, so in exchange for returning to Becky and me our lives, it took two others. You may not have been aware of it, but in saving Becky's life, Don Carlos gave up his. In the end, and when it really counted, he proved he loved his granddaughter and his family. Despite his wretched sins, he died a hero.

The second life fate took that day was Sadie Thompson's. At the time the earthquake struck, Sadie was sitting on the boulder, pulling her loot from the old hollow tree. The tree was rotten, and it collapsed from the violent shaking, crushing Sadie.

Isa and José were married soon after. It was a simple ceremony. Becky was the maid of honor, and I was best man. Don Carlos hadn't disinherited Isa after all. He left her financially secure, but Tere inherited the house, the vineyards, and the winery. Tere, however, was busy with other interests (It will please you to know that she became a suffragette and a great political influence in Northern California.), so she asked José to run the winery. He, Isa, and Becky lived in the mansion, and he managed the estate and the winery. They cared lovingly for Doña Ana until she died.

Isa's mental health improved, but she was never completely well. She continued to suffer from episodes of manic depression. José and Becky were a great comfort to her.

When Tere found out about my dream to become a doctor, she insisted on sending me to school right away. She even offered to pay for my entire education. I only agreed when she promised to let me pay back every penny when I could afford to.

Becky and I were officially engaged when she turned seventeen, but we didn't marry until I finished medical school. Our son was born rather late in our lives. Jason was a blessing. He decided on his own to follow in my footsteps and become a physician.

I invested wisely, thanks to your stock tips, and became

very wealthy. Since I already felt like the richest man on Earth, after all you had given Becky and me, I did not need more money. So after I repaid Tere, I kept the silent promise I had made to you many years before. I am using the money I receive from my many investments to create the best trauma and head-injury clinic on the West Coast. Built in the county of your accident, it will be waiting for you in 1996. I have named it the Rebecca Lee Winthrop Memorial Hospital, in her memory and, secretly, in yours. My beloved Becky died of cancer five years ago.

Jason has promised to continue in my efforts after I am gone. Other than Magda and me, no one knew about your trips to the past until I confided in Jason. You can well imagine how difficult it was to make him believe. I'm not entirely sure he does believe, but he trusts me. And whatever the reason, I know he'll work to make the clinic the best possible. Jason's daughter, Theresa, is three years old. Who knows? Perhaps she, too, will choose to carry on the Winthrop tradition.

So, as you see, my dear Allison, things have come full circle. What you gave to me, I have tried to give back to you. If this letter reaches you, we have completed a circle of time. I pray we meet again, in a time and place that is ours.

Your loving and faithful friend,
Joshua Winthrop